Lunchbox and the Aliens

Lunchbox
and the
Aliens

Bryan W. Fields

ILLUSTRATIONS BY
Kevan Atteberry

HENRY HOLT AND COMPANY

NEW YORK

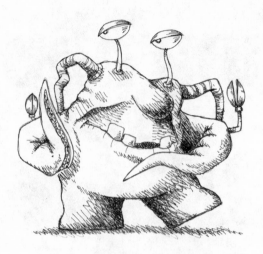

Henry Holt and Company, LLC
Publishers since 1866
175 Fifth Avenue
New York, New York 10010
www.henryholtchildrensbooks.com

Henry Holt® is a registered trademark of Henry Holt and Company, LLC.
Text copyright © 2006 by Bryan W. Fields
Illustrations copyright © 2006 by Kevan Atteberry
Distributed in Canada by H. B. Fenn and Company Ltd.

Library of Congress Cataloging-in-Publication Data
Fields, Bryan W.
Lunchbox and the aliens / Bryan W. Fields; illustrations by Kevan Atteberry—1st ed.
p. cm.
Summary: Lunchbox is an ordinary basset hound until he is abducted by aliens,
zapped by a mental enhancer, and sent back to convert Earth's garbage into food—
a task that would be easier if he had opposable thumbs, or at least tentacles.
ISBN-13: 978-0-8050-7995-1
ISBN-10: 0-8050-7995-5
[1. Basset hound—Fiction.   2. Dogs—Fiction.
3. Extraterrestrial beings—Fiction.   4. Inventions—Fiction.
5. Humorous stories.   6. Science fiction.] I. Atteberry, Kevin, ill.   II. Title.
PZ7.F47916Lun 2006   [Fic]dc22   2005026580

First Edition—2006 / Designed by Amy Ryan
Printed in the United States of America on acid-free paper. ∞

1   3   5   7   9   10   8   6   4   2

To Berniece Rabe,
who believed from the start
—B. W. F.

Lunchbox and the Aliens

Lunchbox rolled happily in the grass, squirming from side to side like a sausage heating unevenly. He paused occasionally, allowing the June sun to warm one side or the other, and letting his long ears flop over his face or spread out flat on the ground. Then he resumed, grunting and snorting in pure canine contentment, oblivious to the mailman, oblivious to fleas, oblivious to the alien eyes that observed him from two hundred miles up.

Aboard the Scwozzwort exploration vessel *Urplung Greebly*, Frazz attempted to give an order. "Increase magnification," he squeaked, sounding nothing like a ship's commander. He knew the order would be ignored anyway.

"*Uhhhhhhhp,*" belched Grunfloz. "It's up all the way, *sir*." Grunfloz always managed to make "sir" sound like an insult. After fifteen years alone with Frazz, he meant it with all of his hearts.

"Well, I couldn't tell, you've gotten so much slime all over the screen," whined Frazz. He shuddered at the hideous creature displayed on the console.

"I like it," said Grunfloz. He tapped the view screen with a tentacle, smearing a small winged specimen from Gangus Five that had been attracted by the light.

Frazz gagged as he watched Grunfloz lick his tentacle. Of all the disgusting life-forms they had encountered across the galaxy, Grunfloz was still the grossest of them all. He was huge, nearly twice as big as Frazz, and seldom used the body sanitizer.

"I think I'm going to pick this one up," said Grunfloz.

"Oh no you're not!" shouted Frazz. "We have more than enough specimens loose as it is! The whole ship is filthy with them! We've got slime molds from the moons of Karkoran! Spit-bugs from Orknalia! Walking carnivorous plants from the Woofoo sector! They're breeding in the *froonga* rations, they're fighting in the ductwork, and . . . and"—Frazz felt his head tendrils starting to warm up, turning from dull green to a sort of burnt orange that became brighter at the tips—"that little oozy thing from Furporis Twelve—"

"—is building a nest in your quarters, yes, I know, *sir*." Grunfloz smiled, a sarcastic grin that spread all the way across his belly, exposing grungy yellow teeth. "You know, I think it likes you. Now, if you'll excuse me, *sir*, I'll just go and prepare the capture bay."

"No you will not!" shouted Frazz. Much to his delight, Grunfloz noticed that Frazz's head tendrils were now bright orange from base to tip. He woggled his eyestalks at Frazz and sneered.

"And who's going to stop me?"

"Grunfloz! I order you not to pick that thing up!"

Grunfloz paused for a moment, scrunching his mouth into a thinking position. One of his eyestalks bobbed toward a lever on the control panel. A slight smirk started from the corner of his mouth.

Frazz backed away, waving his now orange-tinted tentacles. "No! No! Not the gravity generator! It'll make me *rurfroo*—"

Grunfloz gleefully looped a tentacle around the lever and flipped it to the *off* position. Both of them immediately began floating, along with all of the other junk and stray specimens that Grunfloz had collected.

"Eeeeeeep! Grunfloz! You are hereby confined to your quarters!"

"Fine, then, *sir*, I'll just go now." Grunfloz used his huge round feet to push himself off from the control panel toward the exit, being sure to give Frazz a good spin on the way out.

Frazz tumbled end over end, tentacles and head tendrils flailing. "No! Wait! Turn it back on! Grunflozzzz! Come back here, you *gargafron*!"

2

"**O**h no, my baby!"

Lunchbox the Wonder Dog had seen the little girl toddle into the street even before her mother screamed. He heard the aging garbage truck's failing brakes squeal as the driver frantically tried to stop in time. In an instant Lunchbox dashed into the street, seized the child by her romper, and pulled her out of the way as the truck screeched past. After flipping the giggling baby onto his back, he trotted back to the sidewalk, where her grateful mother retrieved her.

"Oh, thank you, Lunchbox!" she said tearfully.

"All in a day's work," said the Wonder Dog's young

owner, Nate Parker. "Come on, Lunchbox, let's go." They continued their walk down Mill Ferron's main street. Suddenly Lunchbox's ears perked up. He sprinted a half-block to the source of the commotion and stretched his long low body across the doorway of the jewelry store. Just then a masked man carrying a gun and a canvas bag dashed out, tripped over the dog, and hit the sidewalk face-first. Jewels and money spilled onto the sidewalk. Nate caught up in time to retrieve the bag's contents and hand them to the store owner while a policeman hand-cuffed the unconscious robber.

"He did it again!" said the officer. "Son, that dog is amazing!"

"Just doing his duty," said Nate calmly. He blushed slightly when the jewelry store owner rewarded him with a hundred-dollar bill, and again when the news photographer snapped their picture. Lunchbox fell into step at Nate's side as they resumed their walk, while the crowd chanted *Go, Lunchbox. Go, Lunchbox* . . .

". . . and this is Lunchbox saving a baby's life, and this one here is him catching a robber, and this is him flying a spaceship."

Nate waved the crayon drawings uncomfortably close to his dad's face. Mr. Parker gently pushed them away and tried to focus on the newspaper in his lap.

"That's nice, Nate, but Lunchbox is just a basset

hound. Nothing but bone between the ears." He glanced through the window at Lunchbox snoozing in the yard amid the scattered contents of Mrs. Giggelberger's garbage can. "He's not Rin-Tin-Tin."

"Who?"

"Never mind. It was before your time."

"You mean like when there was only one channel?"

"There were three." Mr. Parker sighed. "Please, Nate, no more questions right now. I've got a headache."

"But do you like my drawings?" pleaded Nate.

"Yes, they're . . . um . . ." Nate's father took the pictures and quickly pretended to look through them. "They're fine. Nice colors. Now please go back to what you were doing, Son." He handed the sheaf of construction paper back to Nate and rose from his chair.

"Connie, what time did Durwood say he was coming over?"

"He's on his way now," said Mrs. Parker.

Mr. Parker tossed the newspaper onto the recliner and rubbed the back of his neck. He started pacing around the living room.

"Working me to death at the office all day isn't enough for him. He has to come to my house, too. He must think I'm a chump."

"You're not a chump, honey."

"Dad, what's a chump?" Nate looked up from his crayons and paper.

"It's a . . . never mind, Nate. No more questions, just . . . just draw your pictures and don't interrupt, please."

"It's someone who doesn't think for himself, sweetie," said Nate's mother. "Your father is not a chump. Mayor Thornhill could never run his business without him." She kissed her husband on the cheek and placed a plate of fruit on the table.

Mr. Parker shook his head. "Only a chump would do so much for so little."

"Then demand a raise," she said. "Tell him you've got a better offer somewhere else."

"But I don't *have* a better offer. At the moment I'm one of the few people in Mill Ferron lucky enough to even have a *job*."

The warmth left Mrs. Parker's face. "Then *create* one! You have loads of talent. Market your inventions! We can get by on my teaching salary. I'll teach summer school if necessary."

"But you wanted to be home with Nate this summer." Mr. Parker headed for the den. Mrs. Parker's eyes flashed angrily. She started to speak to her husband's back when the doorbell rang. She took a deep breath, briefly fiddled with her bangs, and opened the door, forcing a cheery smile.

"Hi, Durwood, come on in!"

Mayor Thornhill filled the doorway with his huge

frame. He stuck out his hammy hand and smiled broadly. Nate had never seen such enormous teeth on anything with two legs.

"Always a pleasure, Connie, always a pleasure. I know Gerald is a great employee because he has the support of a great wife."

Muffled coughing sounds came from the den.

"Gerry? Durwood's here." Mrs. Parker started toward the den.

"Oh, don't bother, Connie, I can find it on my own. I have some good news for him." Thornhill stepped past her and lumbered toward the den. He smiled at Nate as he passed.

"Looks like you're a real artist there, Nat."

"*Nate*," corrected Mrs. Parker.

"That's right, I'm sorry. *Nate*." Mayor Thornhill continued toward the den and barged through the door.

"He never gets my name right," mumbled Nate. "Dad's right, he's a jerk."

"Nate, you know that's not nice," said his mother, though it was clear from her expression that she agreed with him. "It's time to clean your things off the table so we can eat."

Nate had almost finished cramming the last of his crayons back into the box—they never seemed to go back in as easily as they came out—when the den's door opened. As the two men came out, Mayor Thornhill said something about "really sticking it to Carson." Mr. Parker smiled weakly and nodded his head. Mrs. Parker came from the kitchen again.

"The casserole is done," she said, with forced politeness. "Stay for dinner?" Mr. Parker shot her an exasperated look. Mayor Thornhill paused for a moment, then looked at his watch.

"You know I'd love to, but . . . places to go, people to see. No rest for the weary!" He opened the front door, and then smiled at Mr. Parker.

"You'll have that proposal ready tomorrow, right?"

"Uh . . . yeah, sure thing, boss."

"I always know I can count on you, Gerald. Must be the influence of your darling bride here." He waved at Nate. "See you later, Nat!"

As soon as the door closed, Mrs. Parker folded her arms and raised her eyebrows, grateful that the mayor was gone, but annoyed at having needlessly prepared a big dinner.

"So what's the good news? Did you get a raise?"

"Not exactly."

"Then what?"

"He wants me to be his campaign manager."

"And . . . ?"

He looked at her sheepishly and sighed, his palms

spread out in a helpless gesture. Mrs. Parker leaned forward, hoping that Nate wouldn't hear.

"Chump," she whispered.

Out in the front yard, no one noticed as a shaft of bright light surrounded Lunchbox and pulled him two hundred miles up into the sky.

3

Frazz moaned softly, wincing as he lifted himself off his couch. The relaxation modulator shut itself off with a long groan, as if exhausted from the effort. He rubbed his eyestalks with aching tentacles. Since he was ignoring the oozy thing from Furporis Twelve nesting above his couch, he didn't see it wave to him as he left his quarters and stepped onto the bridge, which, as usual, was a mess. He hoped Grunfloz wasn't going to pick up that nasty thing they had been watching on the planet.

He was too late.

"Eeeeeeeee! You disobeyed my orders—*again!*" He

gasped for breath, fighting the urge to *rurfroo* at the horrid sight before him.

It looked like nothing they had ever seen, and sprawled out on the deck of the capture bay, it was even uglier than it had appeared on their view screen.

"I hope it's still alive," said Grunfloz, cautiously poking it with his tentacle.

"Grunfloz! Ewwww! Don't touch it! Think of the biohazard!" Frazz realized how silly that sounded—Grunfloz was worse than any biohazard *he* could imagine.

"Relax; I've scanned it, *sir*. Nothing that wouldn't take less than three weeks to incubate. You're fine for now."

"Eeeeeep!" squealed Frazz, who ran to use his body sanitizer.

"That was easy," said Grunfloz to himself. He pulled a *froonga* stick from his stash and chewed thoughtfully, unaware of the crumbs falling to the deck in front of him. His eyestalks bobbed as he inspected the creature. Long body, short legs. At the sides of what Grunfloz assumed was its head, two large, loose flaps of skin flopped uselessly. Maybe some sort of wings? Could this species have once had the ability to fly? He grinned at the thought of Frazz in a ship full of these things flying around.

🪐 🪐 🪐

Lunchbox stirred slightly. His stomach told him it was time to get some dinner before his next nap. He opened one eye carefully, then suddenly jerked his head up and looked around in confusion. This was not home. Everything smelled different. Instinctively he put his nose down to get his bearings. The ground was cold and hard, with a completely unfamiliar smell.

He sniffed his way around in the dim light, whimpering softly. As his confusion began to mount, he became more agitated, panting as he whined. Something near him moved. Lunchbox tried to focus his eyes on the movement, while his nose zeroed in on a particularly strong odor, definitely something rotten. Garbage, maybe? He wagged his tail in anticipation, his mouth watering. He sniffed the cold surface again, bumped against something small and crumbly, and licked his nose. Yummy! Sort of like . . . moldy cheese . . . with a hint of old sneakers. He moved forward . . . another morsel . . . and another. He decided that whatever this place was, it was fine with him!

Grunfloz watched in fascination as the creature gobbled up the *froonga* crumbs on the deck. Moving slowly, staying in the shadows, he carefully broke off a large piece of the *froonga* stick and tossed it past the creature. As soon as the food hit the surface, the creature was on it, snarfing it down so quickly and noisily that Grunfloz smiled, momentarily reminded of his relatives back home. He slowly extended the whole stick toward the animal. It growled, but stopped when it recognized the food. It began to drool. Grunfloz smiled again. I like this thing, he thought.

Nate grabbed Lunchbox's dish from the kitchen floor and filled it with dry dog food. It smelled like meat-flavored breakfast cereal. With a little warm water added, it smelled like meat-flavored breakfast cereal that was going to get soggy really fast, just the way Lunchbox liked it.

"Mom, have you seen Lunchbox?"

"He's probably just out sniffing around the neighborhood. Leave his food on the front porch and he'll be home in a flash. You can set your watch by his stomach." Mrs. Parker turned her attention back to the broccoli she was pulling from the steamer.

Broccoli, yuck, thought Nate. I'd rather have dog food.

"It's got to be around here somewhere," Frazz muttered to himself. "I know I packed it when we left on this stupid mission." His once-pristine quarters were a wreck. Scattered across the deck, spilling out of their storage compartments, were dozens of learning modules. Frazz picked them up one at a time, frantically read their titles, and tossed them on the deck again, growing more frustrated with each one.

The hatch to his quarters slid open, startling him. Grunfloz sauntered in, grinning as he bobbed his eyestalks around the room.

"I love what you've done with the place. Looks real homey, *sir.*"

"You're supposed to request permission," barked Frazz. "You *know* that!"

Grunfloz feigned an apologetic look. He made a big show of snapping to attention, smoothing his head tendrils, and straightening his eyestalks.

"Lowly Enlisted Scwozzwort Third Class Grunfloz requests permission to enter the captain's quarters, *SIR!*" he barked.

"Request denied. Go away!"

Grunfloz smirked and reached up above the bulkhead to pat the oozy thing from Furporis Twelve, then wiped his tentacle on the wall. Frazz slumped on the deck, eyeing the pile in front of him.

"What do you *want*, Grunfloz? I'm busy."

"Oh, nothing." Grunfloz picked up a learning module and looked at the title. "Hmm . . . *How to Be a Malfurbum Gwealfee.*"

"It doesn't say that!" snapped Frazz.

"Does too."

"Give me that!" Frazz snatched the module from Grunfloz's grip. "It says *Principles of Command for Effective Superior Officers.*" It was the one he had been looking for.

Snickering, Grunfloz planted himself on Frazz's couch and leaned back. "Still trying to use those learning modules, huh? Face it, they just don't work on you."

"GO AWAY!" Frazz slammed the module into the mental enhancer and grabbed the helmet from its holder. "NOW!"

"You're supposed to say 'dismissed.' Enjoy your learning session, *sir.*" Grunfloz saluted the little oozy thing on his way out. It chortled affectionately. Frazz tried to ignore it and put the helmet on, a little too hard, pinching his swollen head tendrils.

He flopped onto his couch, and then realized in horror that Grunfloz had just been sitting there. Dropping the helmet on the floor, he ran to his body sanitizer and quickly climbed in, slamming the hatch shut.

A large black snuffling object appeared at the cabin's entrance. *Sniff, sniff, snorf.* More interesting smells to investigate. Keeping its nose close to the deck, the thing from the planet below plodded slowly inside, quietly encouraged by Grunfloz, who leaned against the wall in the outside corridor, tossing chunks of *froonga* into the open hatch and smiling wickedly. It sniffed the device lying on the deck. Grunfloz tossed another chunk, which landed inside the helmet. The creature quickly stuck its head in to retrieve it.

At first Frazz didn't notice the power drain in the body sanitizer, assuming that the flickering lights were just from his agitated brain. It was not until he heard the racket outside that he realized something else was wrong.

He popped the door open to see Grunfloz's latest specimen with its head stuck squarely in the mental enhancer's helmet. The creature convulsed wildly as little bolts of energy flickered around its body.

Grunfloz yanked it free while Frazz gaped in horror.

"You *idiot!*" Frazz screamed. "What are you trying to do?"

Grunfloz hastily checked the stunned animal for signs of life. A piece of *froonga* dangled from its jaws. Frazz hoped it was dead, and was disappointed when it stirred, and even more so when it sucked the *froonga* into its mouth and began chewing.

Grunfloz sighed with relief, then pointed his eyestalks angrily at Frazz.

"What are *you* trying to do? You leave this dangerous equipment lying around while you take another beauty bath? You could have killed it!"

"Get out of my quarters! And take that disgusting thing with you!"

Grunfloz cradled the creature in his tentacles and cooed softly to it. "Don't mind him. He's just a *malfurbum gwealfee.*"

Frazz turned so orange he thought his head tendrils would ignite. "GET OUT!" he shouted.

"With pleasure," muttered Grunfloz. "Come on, little friend, let's go."

5

"**Y**ou can use my desk while I'm at lunch, Nate," said Alice, the secretary. She made sure that there was plenty of scratch paper for him to doodle on while his dad worked in his cubicle nearby. "And you can use these, too." She placed a coffee can full of colored markers and highlighters in front of him and hurried out.

Nate fingered the markers sticking out of the can. Normally he would have dumped them all on the desk and began sketching a new adventure for Lunchbox, but he couldn't, not today. The previous evening he'd called and called for Lunchbox, ridden his bike all over the neighborhood until dark, and then enlisted his dad to drive around in the minivan, shining a flashlight into people's yards in the hope that his dog was sniffing through their garbage, or maybe visiting other dogs. They even went door-to-door until it was too late to knock, but no one had seen Lunchbox.

He rested his chin on his hands and sighed. Why had he thought it would be interesting to visit Dad at work? Still, it was close to lunchtime. A chance for hamburgers and ice cream, assuming his father would ever come out of his cubicle for a breath of fresh air.

Nate looked up just as an apelike man entered the office. Leland Purvis, head of Purvis Sanitation. With his shaved head and thick neck, he just didn't look right wearing a suit. Mr. Purvis glanced around warily. Unable to see any grown-ups, he fastened his beady eyes on Nate at the reception desk.

"I'm here ta see Mayor Thornhill."

"I'll let him know you're here." Nate quickly punched the intercom button on Alice's speakerphone.

"Mr. Thornhill, Mr. Purvis is here to see you."

Thornhill's voice crackled over the speakerphone. "Send him in."

Purvis grunted. His bulldog face showed no hint of a smile until he pulled open the door to Thornhill's office.

"Mr. Mayor, how ya doin'," he blurted, closing the door behind him.

"I got your message," said Thornhill flatly.

"And?" said Purvis. The voices came through the speaker at Alice's desk; Mayor Thornhill had apparently forgotten to turn off his intercom.

"There are some problems with your service."

"Whaddaya mean?" Purvis sounded angry and scared at the same time.

Nate carefully picked up the handset so his father wouldn't hear him eavesdropping.

"Well, let's see, here . . ." Nate heard desk drawers opening and papers shuffling. "Here's a letter from Mrs. Edith Giggelberger, complaining that your guys never come at the same time—she never knows when to put her trash out. When she puts it out early, your guys come late and the neighbor's dog gets into it!"

Nate winced. He knew who the dog was.

"Well, ya know, some days we got more garbage than others," said Mr. Purvis.

"You're sloppy." Thornhill thumped his fingers on the desk in rhythm with each word. "Give me one good reason why we should renew your contract."

Purvis was silent for a moment, but then he spoke with an air of certain victory.

"I got ten good reasons, as in, 10 percent."

"Is that so." The mayor didn't sound impressed. Nate heard more paper rustling. "This is a bid from your competition."

Purvis grunted. "You ain't gonna let the city council see that one, for sure. With a bid that low, your cut ain't gonna be that much."

"Maybe, maybe not. Their bid also includes automated pickup. They can do the same job with a third as many guys as you can in your beat-up old trucks."

Purvis breathed a little harder. "You don't want news about this to leak, Mr. Mayor. One word to the city council an' your reelection goes down the tubes!"

"You're forgetting who got you this sweet deal, aren't you? One word to your parole officer, and you're back in the slammer again."

"Even you couldn't do that," snarled Purvis.

"Let's see now . . . attempting to bribe a public official . . . operating a sanitation business without proper permits . . ."

"I got permits!"

"You do . . . *for now.*" Thornhill's chair squeaked, like he was leaning back feeling satisfied. "Don't forget who helped you *get* those permits."

Purvis mumbled some words that Nate had heard on cable TV once when his parents thought he was asleep. "Okay. I can only go up to 11 percent."

"Fifteen. And get some of those automatic Dumpster things."

"You're killin' me! How'm I gonna pay you 15 percent and still upgrade my trucks? It's 11 or nothin'."

"Raise your bid to cover a couple of new trucks. I'll sell the idea to the city council. Your competition will go back in my desk here, and the city council will never see it. Thirteen percent."

"Twelve. Them trucks ain't cheap."

"But you can fire most of those knot-heads on your crew, Leland. Thirteen."

Nate could almost hear the gears squeaking in Purvis's greedy head.

"Twelve and a half. Gladys wants to go to Graceland this year."

Thornhill chuckled. "Fine with me. I'll put in a good word for you at the bank."

Nate heard a briefcase popping open, followed by more shuffling sounds. "That's half of it," said Purvis. "Twenties and hundreds. You'll get the other half when the city pays its bill."

"Fair enough," said Thornhill.

"You can count it if you need to."

"No need, Leland. This is a relationship based on *trust*."

"Yes, sir." Purvis chuckled. "Complete trust."

Nate quickly busied himself with the markers as the two men came out of the office. Mayor Thornhill was stuffing something in his suit pocket, smiling like a well-fed shark.

"Leland, thanks for stopping by." He smiled until Purvis left, then frowned as he walked over to Mr. Parker's cubicle.

"You got that proposal ready, Gerry?" Nate hated that. Only Mom and Grandma were allowed to call his father Gerry.

"Working on it now," said Mr. Parker.

"I really needed that done today! You said you'd get right on it last night."

"I did. Just didn't . . . didn't have time to finish it. My son's dog disappeared and we were up half the night looking for him."

"We're not going to let a dog get in the way of our campaign, now, are we? I need you to focus on it. Don't let Carson get a head start." He straightened his coat, unconsciously patting the lump in his pocket. "I've got to take care of some business at city hall. Call me if you have any questions."

Thornhill paused as he passed the reception desk. "Nat," he said, making a sad face. "Sorry to hear about your dog. I hope you find him."

Nate mumbled some thanks but kept his eyes down. *The mayor is a crook, and Dad doesn't know it,* he thought.

Malfurbum gwealfee . . . MALFURBUM GWEAL-FEE . . .

Frazz stared glumly at the mental enhancer. No way was he going to use it now, not without a thorough decontamination first.

Grunfloz dared to call me a *malfurbum gwealfee.*

His thoughts crawled back fifteen years to that fateful day in his commander's office . . . He could still see it. Commander Narzargle's head tendrils were bright orange. His body seemed almost to split in half as he opened his belly wide to roar at Frazz.

"Sub-Junior Deputy Accounting Officer Frazz!" he

bellowed. "Do you realize the magnitude of your STUPIDITY?"

Frazz's eyestalks hung in shame. He looked at the floor, wishing he could melt into it, as the commander continued.

"How do you explain how you managed to sell forty-three *Urplung*-class ships to the Hoofonoggles for the *price of a sack of moldy* froonga *sticks*?" Narzargle slammed his tentacles on his control console, clamped his belly shut, and glared at Frazz, stretching his eyestalks to their limits.

"I . . . I was . . . I didn't know . . . I hit the Send button without knowing that the numbers were backward . . . sir. . . ."

Another wave of bright orange pulsed through the commander's head tendrils. "YOU . . . DIDN'T . . . KNOW! You . . . you are a . . ." The commander trailed off, not wanting to utter the dreaded words. "You are a . . . *malfurbum gwealfee.*"

"No!" Frazz cried in horror. "No, please, no-o-o!" He covered his eyestalks with his tentacles and sobbed.

Commander Narzargle sighed deeply. "I can recommend only one punishment."

"You . . . you don't mean the . . ." Frazz squeaked.

"The *eebeedee.*"

Frazz gasped for breath. The *eebeedee*, the official embarrassment ceremony, the ultimate punishment. He would be set on a cart at the head of a long procession through the main streets, draped in the *yakayaka*, or "robe of stupidity." The crowd would chant, softly at first, then louder and faster, *malfurbum gwealfee . . . malfurbum gwealfee . . .* At the height of the ceremony the *yakayaka* would be torn from his body and he would be pelted with rotten garbage, then forced to spend his life begging in the streets for *froonga* crumbs, performing the Dance of Stupidity while singing:

> *I'm malfurbum gwealfee, won't you please feed me*
> *I used to have a name, now I am full of shame*
> *Tell your children not to look*
> *At my face that's full of gook*
> *Rurfroo, rurfroo, give me some crumbs!*

The horror of it was too much for young Frazz. "Please, sir. Can't you just kill me instead?"

"I wish I could," snarled the commander. "Oh, how I wish I could. I would do it ever so slowly, with my bare tentacles. Twice, even." Narzargle aimed his eyestalks at the ceiling and sighed. "If only it were a perfect universe." He fastened his glare upon Frazz again. "I would almost rather suffer the *eebeedee* myself than tell you what I have been ordered to tell you."

"Sir? You . . . you mean . . . it gets even worse?"

"Oh, how I wish . . ." The commander screwed his mouth up tight and tugged at his head tendrils. "The

Hoofonoggles . . . have declared you . . . an *honorary citizen* of their world."

"I—I don't understand, sir."

"It means you're their hero, you twit!" Narzargle spat. "The Hoofonoggle ambassador is waiting outside to award you the 'Medal of Generosity.' "

"The medal of . . ."

"Generosity! Thanks to your *narf*-brained error that cost Central Command nearly one year's revenue, the Hoofonoggles have adopted you as one of their own! And thanks to the Treaty of Roogah, we have promised not to harm any citizen of Hoofonogglia, not even the honorary ones!" Narzargle turned to stare out of his office porthole.

"You mean . . . I'm . . . I'm free?" squeaked Frazz.

Commander Narzargle turned around slowly, an evil smile growing on his belly.

"Not exactly."

Frazz shuddered again at the memory. The alternative was almost as bad as the *eebeedee*. A promotion. His own command—the *Urplung Greebly*, last and leakiest of the *Urplung*-class ships. A crew—Grunfloz, formerly a hazardous garbage sorter at the central *froonga* processing plant. And a forty-year exploration mission across the galaxy and back.

When Grunfloz entered Frazz's quarters again, he

found him locked inside the body sanitizer. He yanked it open and stuck a greasy tentacle inside.

"There's something you need to see, *sir*."

"Aaaagh! Grunfloz! Haven't I had enough of you today?"

"You *really* need to see this." Grunfloz dragged him out of the chamber.

"Ow! Ow! Let me go!"

"Hurry up!" Grunfloz set him on his feet and pushed him toward the hatch.

Frazz slapped at Grunfloz with his tentacles. "I'm hurrying, quit shoving!"

They halted just outside of the bridge.

"Look at that!" said Grunfloz triumphantly.

Frazz peered through the entrance. Everything was in its normal foul-smelling disarray, except for one thing.

The creature from the planet was perched on Frazz's command couch.

"Arrrrgh! It's in my seat!" Frazz started to enter the bridge to shoo it away. A huge tentacle blocked his path.

"But look what it's *doing*!" said Grunfloz excitedly. "Look!"

The Scwozzworts watched as the creature used its feet and nose to work the buttons at the command console. The ship's schematics appeared as three-dimensional images above it. The animal scanned them one by one until it seemed to find what it was looking for. Hopping down from the seat, it moved toward the hatchway where the Scwozzworts stood and trotted past them, giving them a slight sniff.

"It's a spy!" cried Frazz. "Shove it out of the air lock!"

"No, it isn't, *sir*. It's *learning*. That jolt from your mental enhancer went right to its brain! It's learning how the ship operates!" Grunfloz was delighted. "Fantastic!"

"But that's *impossible*! It's not even the smartest life-form on that planet down there! It . . . it . . ."

Grunfloz hurried to follow the creature.

"It's not fair," whined Frazz, waddling after him.

Halting outside of the cargo bay, they poked their eyestalks inside the entrance.

The creature moved among the containers strewn about. Various icky life-form specimens frolicked near the main hold, then scattered as the creature approached. It sniffed each door until it found the compartment it was looking for. Rising up on its hind legs, it pressed the keypad several times with a front foot.

"It's using my command code! I told you it was a spy!" wailed Frazz.

"It was your learning module—your code was included with it," Grunfloz said as the enormous door to the compartment hissed open.

"That's our *froonga* storage!" cried Frazz.

The creature suddenly started making loud noises.

"Arrrrrrf! Arrrrrrf!" Frazz began to run, thinking it was about to attack. Grunfloz stopped him.

"It's trying to tell us something!" Grunfloz moved closer to the compartment. Thousands of little yellow specimens scurried out. Thousands more were munching on what was left of—

"—our *froonga*! It's gone!" shouted Frazz. "Your stupid specimens have eaten everything! We're going to starve! You and your 'scientific curiosity'!" He collapsed into a blubbering puddle on the deck.

Grunfloz studied the infested cargo hold, and then looked at the creature. He folded his tentacles and thought for a moment.

"Relax, *sir*. I have an idea. . . ."

Nate punched at his pillow, trying to make it more comfortable. Finally he gave up and tossed it on the floor. He sat back against the headboard and pulled his knees up to his chest, staring at the closet door across the room. One of his favorite drawings was taped to it, the X-29½ Space Fighter. Its pilot was none other than Captain Lunchbox, identified by the big black nose protruding from the helmet inside the canopy. Orange and red laser beams shot from the wings of the ship, destroying fighters piloted by evil mutant cats.

All afternoon he'd tacked up the MISSING BASSET HOUND flyers that his mother had printed for him. Dad

never took his lunch break; Mayor Thornhill seemed intent on working him to death. Not only did Nate miss out on burgers and ice cream, but he couldn't talk to his dad about the conversation he'd overheard. His mother was no less busy, and had only paused her phone conversation long enough to hand Nate the flyers and shoo him out the door.

His wrist and elbow ached from using his dad's staple gun to tack the flyers onto every neighborhood telephone pole. More painful, however, was the thought that he might never see his dog again. They'd been together as far back as Nate could remember. Without Lunchbox there would be no more fantasies to draw, no more adventures to create. No wet cold nose snuffling under his arm to tell him it was feeding time. No sitting on the front steps drinking root beer, giving him belly rubs and watching his hind legs twitch. *Lunchbox, where are you?*

"Grunfloz, that's the stupidest plan you've come up with yet." Frazz waved his eyestalks in disgust. "Even if you don't end up killing it, it won't get any smarter. That was just a freak accident."

"I've scanned the creature's entire neurological system. For reasons I can't explain just yet, it's completely receptive to the mental enhancer, more than any normal Scwozzwort could ever hope to be."

"That's because its brain has plenty of room," huffed Frazz. "It's dumber than an Orknalian spit-bug."

"Do you have a better plan, *sir*?"

Frazz didn't say anything, but a twinge of orange showed at the tip of his head tendrils.

"I didn't think so," said Grunfloz. "Now, I've taken your mental enhancer and made some flow adjustments. It shouldn't stun the creature this time."

"Why do we have to use *my* equipment for this? Why can't we use yours?"

"Because if it breaks, it won't be any great loss. It never works on you anyway."

Frazz looked again at the creature strapped into his mental enhancer. It seemed to be perfectly content with the process, in spite of having been nearly fried the last time. That proved that it was completely stupid and had already forgotten its near-death experience.

"Give me that learning module there," said Grunfloz, pointing.

"*Basics of Froonga Manufacturing*," read Frazz. "This is unbelievable."

"Just give it here, sir!" Grunfloz snatched it from Frazz's grip and popped it into the mental enhancer. He took a deep breath and switched on the device. "Here goes."

The creature sat very still, occasionally blinking its eyes as the current slowly increased. After a few minutes a light flashed to indicate that it was finished. Grunfloz studied the scanning screen briefly, and then turned to Frazz with a grin.

"It worked," he said. "Take a look."

Frazz stared blankly at the screen. A three-dimensional graphic of the animal's brain showed lots of glowing spots. "So?"

"That means *total absorption*," said Grunfloz excitedly.

"Now let's try Volume Two!" He snatched another module and plugged it in.

Frazz was unimpressed. "This is a complete waste of time and equipment."

"Takes one to know one," muttered Grunfloz as Frazz left the bridge.

Lunchbox felt odd. Somehow this was all becoming more familiar to him, and made more sense all the time. He wondered how he had known how to open the place where all the yummy stuff was kept. He wondered why he seemed to know so much about these strange animals he was with. He wondered how he knew he was wondering.

Grunfloz checked his list of learning modules. In addition to *Principles of Command for Effective Superior Officers* and *Basics of Froonga Manufacturing*, the creature had absorbed *Burfloffle's Compendium of the Scwozzwortian Language*, *The Young Scwozzwort's Guide to Technology*, and *The Encyclopedia of Everything Else*. He unhooked the mental enhancer from the animal and stared curiously.

"Well, creature, what do you think?"

Lunchbox cocked his head. The big smelly animal had just asked him what he thought. An answer formed in his mind. I think you are my friend. He tried to speak but all he could say was "arroohmmm ruff hrrrrr." He tried again. "Owrrr ruff mrrrf."

40

Grunfloz scrunched his mouth quizzically. The creature was trying to speak, but its mouth wasn't designed for Scwozzwortian words.

"If you can understand me, raise your right front foot."

The creature sat down and raised its short leg. Grunfloz smiled broadly.

C'mon, Lunchbox. Shake! Attaboy! Good dog!

Lunchbox lowered his paw. Something very familiar had just happened. What was it? He looked at the big smelly animal. Had it just asked him to . . . *shake*? No, no, it had said "raise your right front foot." Reflexively, he started drooling. After something like this he was supposed to get a . . . a . . . *cookie*! He looked around for a cookie. The big smelly animal spoke again.

"You must be hungry," it said. "We don't have much left, but—here, take this." It offered him a small morsel. Lunchbox snatched it eagerly.

Yummy! *Froonga*-cookie.

Grunfloz patted the creature affectionately.

"You really like *froonga*, don't you?"

The creature *murrrrfed* in agreement. Grunfloz opened his private stash and pointed to its dwindling contents.

"As you already know, we're almost out of it."

The creature cocked its head, listening intently.

"We can't make it aboard the ship," said Grunfloz. "But I believe you can help us get what we need." Grunfloz tried hard to read its expression, alien as it was. He paused, somewhat dramatically, and lowered his eyestalks until they were almost in the creature's face. "Will you help us?"

Lunchbox knew the answer to the big smelly animal's question immediately.

I will help you get more *froonga*-cookies. He *arrrfed* his agreement. *Froonga* is made from garbage, he thought. My planet is full of garbage . . . my planet? My . . . home. Must get . . . home. Must see . . . no, must make *froonga*. *Froonga*-cookies.

"This is terrific!" shouted Grunfloz. He wrapped his tentacles around the creature and hugged it. It waved the long thing at its rear and then rolled onto its back. Grunfloz affectionately rubbed its belly, and watched in fascination as one of its hind legs kicked in the air.

"That's my creature," said Grunfloz. "Frazz is going to hate this. I can't wait!"

Good boy, Lunchbox. Attaboy!

No, wait. The big smelly animal had said, "That's my creature."

Tummy rubs, ooh, ooh. Scratch, scratch. Wag, wag.

Lunchbox tried to sort out his thoughts. Need to make *froonga*-cookies for the big, smelly animal and the little whiny animal . . . need *froonga*. . . . Find garbage. Build machine.

One thought came very strongly to Lunchbox's mind, something from deep inside, something much simpler than the new knowledge that had been crammed into his brain:

I must get home to my boy.

8

"Someone's here to see you," called Nate's mother.

Nate didn't feel like seeing anyone.

"Nate!" She rapped on the door. "You have a visitor." Her voice was singsongy, like when she talked about how good broccoli was.

Nate slowly lifted himself from the bed. The door swung open before he could get to it, and the "visitor" rushed in.

Fifty pounds of slobbering hound bowled him over.

"*Lunchbox!*"

"Arroooo!" barked Lunchbox, wagging his tail so hard that it knocked over Nate's desk chair. Nate hugged him tightly, and then wrestled him to the floor for a belly rub.

"Grunfloz, I still can't believe you think that ugly specimen of yours will help us get more *froonga*. You've returned it to its planet, and we'll never see it again. It'll forget everything, and we'll starve to death."

"Relax, *sir*. Our little friend will come through."

"It won't work," repeated Frazz. "How do we know the creature will find what it needs to make *froonga*?"

"You haven't paid attention to the data. That planet is *loaded* with garbage."

"But how do we know the garbage on that planet isn't toxic?"

"Hey, I'm a professional, remember? I know my garbage."

"But what about materials to make the machine?"

"There's enough technology on this planet to provide everything we need. The creature knows exactly what to look for."

"But how is it going to *build* a *froonga* machine? It doesn't even have any tentacles!"

Grunfloz fiddled with the control panel. "You worry too much."

"If you hadn't picked up that little oozy thing on Furporis Twelve, it would have never unlocked all the specimen cubicles in the first place. As a matter of fact, if you hadn't picked up any of those things, we wouldn't *be* in this mess! This is all *your* fault!"

"We have roughly two weeks' worth of *froonga* left. Three weeks, if I eat your share and let you starve." Grunfloz stuck his eyestalks out. "Do you have a better idea?"

As he hugged his dog, Nate noticed that Lunchbox seemed leaner and more muscular, very unlike his normal flabby self.

"Have you been working out? Or did you just go on a diet?" Nate led him to the kitchen and poured a fresh bowl of meat-flavored nuggets. "I bet you're really hungry!"

Lunchbox sniffed carefully at the food in the bowl.

Froonga? No, wait . . . cookie? *No.* This is . . . I don't know what this is. Not *froonga.* Sniff, sniff. Smells familiar, but . . . ugh.

He nibbled a few nuggets, then sat down to think. I will have to be really hungry before I eat more of this. Time to start working on the plan.

9

Nate enjoyed his dinner that evening. He even choked down some broccoli. After dessert, he curled up on the couch in the den with his drawing pad and crayons. Lunchbox lounged quietly at his side.

Nate's father sat at the computer. Three-dimensional images of a robotic window washer twisted across the screen.

"Dad, how come you keep inventing stuff but don't try to sell it?"

Mr. Parker kept his eyes on the screen. "It's just a hobby."

"Mom says you're a genius. How come you have to work for Mayor Thornhill?"

Mr. Parker took off his glasses and turned toward Nate. "It's a steady job."

"But he's a crook!"

"Nate, that's not a nice thing to say."

"He's taking bribes from Mr. Purvis."

"Whatever gave you that idea?"

"I heard it in his office. They talked about the garbage contract, and Mr. Purvis offered him a percentage—I think it was 12 or 13 or something."

"They could have been talking about anything. Mayor Thornhill does business with a lot of people. I don't think what you heard—*Lunchbox! Get down!*"

Lunchbox stood on his hind legs with his front paws on the desk, looking intently at the computer screen. At Mr. Parker's rebuke, he reluctantly lowered himself to the floor, but kept his eyes on the screen.

"I don't think what you heard was necessarily what you *believe* you heard," concluded Mr. Parker.

Nate shrugged. "Even so . . . I wish you didn't have to work for him. You hate it."

Nate's dad shook his head wearily. "Some things can't be helped, Son." He looked at his project on the screen, made a few more clicks with the mouse, and with a heavy sigh, rose from the desk and headed for the living room.

Nate got up and started to follow him when a noise behind him caught his attention.

Lunchbox sat at the computer, working the mouse with his fat paw to rotate Mr. Parker's drawings. Too surprised to scold him, Nate watched the dog add new shapes to the existing drawing. After a few minutes he found his voice.

"Lunchbox! How . . . what . . . *you can't do that, you're a dog!*" Nate grabbed Lunchbox by his collar, but he wouldn't budge.

"Urrrrrrrrmmmmm," growled Lunchbox.

"That's Dad's file! Get down from there!"

"Urrrrrrf." Lunchbox pointed his nose at the printer. "Hroom arrrf murf."

"That's the printer." Nate couldn't believe he was explaining technical things to his dog.

"Rowwrrrr," said Lunchbox, looking at the screen, then at the printer again. He looked at Nate. "Owr-rrrrrrrrr."

"What, you want to print this? Click here." Nate pointed at the PRINT icon on the toolbar. Lunchbox clumsily moved the cursor and clicked. Nate was horrified.

"No, no! That was the SAVE button! Bad dog!"

Lunchbox whined softly and carefully clicked the PRINT icon.

"Give me that!" hissed Nate. He grabbed the mouse and tried to undo the save while Lunchbox hopped down and waited by the printer stand for the drawing to come out. "I can't change it back! You've ruined it!"

"Ruined *what*?" Mr. Parker's voice behind him nearly made Nate jump out of his socks. "Nate! What are you doing to my project?"

"I didn't do it, Lunchbox did! Something weird's happened! He's smart now!"

"That's ridiculous." Mr. Parker paused, like he was counting to ten in his head. After a deep breath, he continued, his voice a little softer, with a more concerned tone. "It's not like you to be this way." He leaned past

Nate and began deleting Lunchbox's modifications to his drawing. "I know these last couple of days have been hard on you. You're obviously overtired."

Nate groaned to himself. Overtired. The parental explanation for everything. That and "too much sugar." "Yes, officer, we know he's an axe murderer, but, well, he's overtired and had a little too much sugar today."

"Dad, I'm not overtired. And don't say I've had too much sugar."

Mr. Parker raised an eyebrow. "What I think you've had, Son, is too much worrying about your dog. He's home now; he's just fine."

"But he's acting funny. You saw him at the computer earlier."

"He was being his normal nosy self! He wasn't actually *using* it." Mr. Parker finished cleaning up the drawing, saved it, and closed the program. "However, I . . ." He reached down for the drawing hissing from the printer, which made Lunchbox growl softly. "Easy, boy." He patted the dog's ribs, and then waved the drawing in front of Nate. "I don't want any more of this nonsense, understood?"

"Yeah," mumbled Nate. He gathered his drawing pad and crayons. "I'm going to bed now." He watched silently as his dad crumpled the printout and tossed it in the wastebasket by the desk. Lunchbox whimpered.

"Goodnight, Nate." Mr. Parker gestured toward the door, smiling. "Go on, Lunchbox. No more computer for you tonight."

Nate sat up in bed, with the faint light from the partially open door spilling across the sleeping dog at his feet, and wondered. It was just too weird. Lunchbox had changed from a lazy blob to a superdog. And using the computer . . . what could have happened during the last two days?

Maybe Lunchbox had met a witch or a troll that put a spell on him, he thought. No, that's dumb. There's no such thing as magic. There had to be a more scientific explanation. The muscles . . . the brains . . .

"I'll bet," he said out loud, "you dug up something radioactive and it gave you superpowers, like Spider-man. That's a logical explanation." Satisfied with this, Nate settled back and began to feel drowsy.

Lunchbox waited until the boy was asleep, then carefully slipped to the floor and out to the den.

I have work to do. No time for resting, he thought.

10

"**G**runfloz! Why are you eating?" Frazz cried in horror.
"Uh . . . because I was *hungry*?" Grunfloz examined
the half-eaten *froonga* stick in his tentacle, pretending
to debate whether or not to finish it. He shrugged and
popped the remainder into his mouth, chewing with it wide
open so Frazz could see every crumb dissolve on his tongue.

"We've got to ration our supply! You're eating like a
Nooskian *flarmgrok*!"

Grunfloz belched. "Relax. Our experiment is going
just fine."

"*Your* experiment," snapped Frazz. "And it's doomed
to failure."

"It's too bad you feel that way, *sir*. I guess you probably wouldn't be interested in *this*." Grunfloz tapped the viewer. Frazz hesitantly craned his eyestalks toward it.

"What is it?"

"Plans for the *froonga* machine. The creature is working on them right now." Grunfloz carefully pointed out the dim shapes flickering on the screen. "That looks like a *rantis gramulator*."

"A *what*?"

Grunfloz rolled his eyestalks, speaking slowly, but not very patiently. "A *rantis gramulator*. It's the main core of a *froonga* processor. It harnesses *plookie* radiation to transform organic garbage into nutritious *froonga*."

Frazz was astonished, not just because he had no clue what *plookie* radiation was, but because the tiny sensor Grunfloz had implanted in the creature's forehead was working perfectly, recording everything it was seeing. After a long silence he finally thought of something negative to say.

"Those are just plans. It could still take forever to build the machine, assuming it can even find the right technology."

"This planet is covered with *plookie* technology, but the creatures down there apparently don't know what they've got. Look at this." Grunfloz showed a view of the planet, setting the scanners to detect *plookie* radiation. The entire planet glowed with it. "All of their machines—all of their appliances generate *plookie* radiation."

"Is it dangerous?"

"In its unrefined state, it's completely harmless. Once it enters the *rantis gramulator*, though, it becomes highly powerful, and yes, very, very dangerous."

"And you think this stupid creature of yours is going to build a *remus gargonator*, or whatever it is, without blowing up the whole planet."

"*Rantis gramulator*," corrected Grunfloz. "And no, it's not going to blow the planet up. It *could*, of course, if it doesn't get the frequency just right, but I've made sure that doesn't happen."

"How?"

"When the creature finishes the machine, I'll give it this." Grunfloz held up a flat, round module. "This is a *plookie* regulator, tuned to the exact frequency needed for *froonga* processing. Once it attaches this to the *rantis gramulator*, everything else will work."

"What if the creature doesn't install it right? Or if it gets out of adjustment?" Frazz wrapped his tentacles nervously around his head. "Does the planet blow up?"

"With that much *plookie* radiation feeding a chain reaction? Not just the planet, but probably half of the solar system, and us with it," said Grunfloz calmly.

Frazz stared limply at the viewer, then turned his eyestalks toward Grunfloz. "I think I need some *froonga*."

"Help yourself," said Grunfloz, munching another stick.

Lunchbox wandered through the streets with his latest printouts between his teeth, being careful not to slobber on them.

I must find a place to work without interference, he thought.

Some of his four-legged friends called to him from behind fences. Their primitive communication skills were like someone shouting "Hey! Hey! Hey!" for hours on end. He vaguely remembered being like that but found it difficult to believe. He had no time for socializing. He was a dog with a mission.

11

Lunchbox came plodding in just before bedtime, looking very tired. He plopped down on the rug by Nate's bed and went right to sleep.

Saturday morning they awoke at the same time.

"You're not running off today," said Nate. "You're grounded. And stay off of Dad's computer."

Lunchbox yawned and licked his nose a couple of times. He looked hungry.

Nate led him to the kitchen and poured a bowl of dog food. Lunchbox nibbled a few pieces, then belly-flopped on the floor and whimpered.

"Oh, come on! You love this stuff! It's good for you!"

said Nate, sounding uncomfortably like his mother talking about broccoli.

Lunchbox raised his head up and cocked his ears at the sound of banging in the garage.

"That's Dad working on his gadgets," said Nate. "You wanna go see?"

Lunchbox was through the kitchen and pawing at the side door before Nate could move.

"Slow down! It's just Dad!" He eased the door open. The dog slammed through it so hard that the doorknob was wrenched from Nate's fingers.

Inside the garage Lunchbox stopped and gazed, drooling, at the array of technology before him. Several home-built computers and servos whirred and clacked as the various machines responded to Mr. Parker's commands. On one monitor, lines of diagnostic gibberish scrolled endlessly.

Nate tried to be a little less intrusive than Lunchbox. "Hi, Dad."

"Be careful, Son, there's a lot of money tied up in these things. Whoa, Lunchbox! Get away from that or your nose will light up!"

Nate dragged Lunchbox by his collar across the garage floor. "Sit!"

Lunchbox didn't sit. He strained against Nate's grip, anxious to explore all of the things in the garage.

"What's gotten into him?" said Mr. Parker, only glancing in his direction as he tried to solder a capacitor in place.

"You wouldn't believe me if I told you," said Nate, relaxing his grip slightly when Lunchbox finally sat down. "You haven't so far."

Mr. Parker put down the soldering iron and sighed. "If it's about Lunchbox and my computer, you're right."

Nate knew he needed to change the subject. "So what is all this stuff?"

"This thing in front of me is going to be a robotic window washer, as you know." Mr. Parker pointed to a creation in the corner, consisting of a lot of electronics and an old water heater. "That's a—gee, how do I explain that one—it's a hyperbaric laundry sterilizer. Like an autoclave, sort of, but more sophisticated."

"A what?"

"It kills germs in dirty laundry."

"Okay . . . umm, what's that thing?" Nate pointed to a long, boxy machine with a huge snowblower funnel bolted to it.

"That's my pride and joy. You put cement, or wood chips, or whatever, into this end, set the controls here . . ." Mr. Parker leaned over to adjust a lever, and threw a stack of old newspapers into the scoop. "Watch this."

The machine sputtered and coughed, then whirred to

life. It shook violently, scooting around on the floor a few inches. A spring-loaded door opened at the other end, and out slid four neatly compressed paper bricks.

"Wow! That's cool!" said Nate.

"You can use these for firewood, building blocks, insulation, or whatever. Put cement in there, add water, and it makes foundation bricks. It will make bricks out of anything—fertilizer, glass, old shoes—you name it. Organic or not."

"Who would use bricks made of fertilizer?"

"I don't know, but I'm betting somebody could."

Lunchbox gazed at the brick machine, wagging his tail in delight. Panting, he began sniffing around the garage at the other things. More than once, he stuck his slobbering face right into Mr. Parker's lap to see what he was doing, only to be shoved away and scolded again.

Over the next two hours, Lunchbox continually got in the way. Sometimes he stuck his nose in something to sniff it and get a better look, other times he just stared at Nate's dad. This seemed to disturb Mr. Parker more than anything else.

"Nate, would you *please* take him outside? He's driving me nuts!"

"Okay, Dad." Nate dragged the protesting dog to the backyard and shut the door. Lunchbox immediately began howling.

"That's not going to help," said Mr. Parker with a

groan. "Take him somewhere else! Take him for a walk. Take him to the park. Take him *anyplace*!" He picked up a wrench that Lunchbox had drooled on and wiped it with a rag. "Please!"

Lunchbox moped all the way to the park, letting the slack center of the leash, as well as his ears, drag on the sidewalk.

"What's your problem?" said Nate. "You've always liked going to the park. Look, I brought a Frisbee! Maybe

now that you're smart you can catch it like the other dogs." He waved the plastic disk in front of the dog's nose. Lunchbox turned his head away as if Nate had just offered him a dead skunk.

At the park, Lunchbox sat under a tree and watched with total disinterest as other dogs ran and played.

"Watch what they do," said Nate, pointing to a teenaged boy with a hyperactive Jack Russell terrier, which danced around his feet waiting for him to throw a Frisbee. As soon as the disk left the young man's hand, the little dog exploded across the park and caught it a full five feet in the air, performing a graceful pirouette before hitting the ground running. With its prize in its teeth, the dog sprinted back to its owner to repeat the process.

"I bet you could do that with some practice," said Nate. He tried to get Lunchbox worked into a playful mood by waving the disk in his face. "Come on, Lunchbox! Here, look at the Frisbee! C'mon, boy!" Nate made a short, somewhat wobbly throw. The Frisbee arced and came down at a forty-five degree angle into the grass. Lunchbox watched it bounce and roll back toward them. He yawned audibly, then flopped down and whimpered.

"Okay, you stay there, I'll throw it to you, and you catch it in your teeth. It's simple." Nate backed up about twenty feet and threw the Frisbee gently in Lunchbox's direction. It landed with a soft thud in front of him.

Lunchbox blinked and glanced at the terrier going crazy for the object again and again.

If that boy doesn't want the thing, why does that stupid animal keep bringing it back? he wondered.

Nate threw the Frisbee repeatedly toward Lunchbox, shouting encouragement. One shot bounced off of his nose.

Ouch! Why is my boy throwing things at me? I can't concentrate on my calculations.

Nate sat and scratched him behind the ears. "I don't understand. You're the smartest dog in the world, but you can't spend your whole life in front of the computer. You've got to get exercise, too. That's what Mom tells *me*, anyway."

He stroked Lunchbox's ribs and felt the meat that had replaced the flab.

"Well, maybe you're okay on the exercise. I just wish you'd play like other dogs."

Lunchbox stared blankly at the ground, trying to ignore the chattering boy.

I can make a *rantis gramulator* out of all those things at home. I just need a few more things to . . . ooh, ooh . . . please, not now, I'm trying to . . . ooh, ooh, tummy rub!

He rolled over and let the boy rub his belly. His back legs kicked in the air.

I just can't resist tummy rubs.

"Grunfloz, your experiment is loafing!" said Frazz nervously. "Look at the screen!"

Grunfloz studied the images. The creature appeared to be upside down. The sensor indicated a reduction in brain activity, while the creature's pulse, respiration, and saliva production picked up. It was obviously distracted by its two-legged companion.

"We'll have to send it a message," said Grunfloz. "The sensor in its forehead is also a receiver."

Frazz wrapped his tentacles around his face and sighed, looking at the dwindling *froonga* supply. His stomach growled. "Give me that comlink. *I'll* speak to the creature." He thumped the device a couple of times. "Is this thing on?" He grunted for a moment to clear his throat, and then he shouted: "HEY, YOU STUPID ANIMAL! GET BACK TO WORK!"

With a sudden yelp, Lunchbox rolled to his feet. He squinted his eyes, the way a human with a headache might squint in bright sunlight. He shook his head, accidentally slapping Nate with his ears, then stared off into the distance, whimpering slightly. Before Nate could check to see what was wrong, Lunchbox sprinted away, crossing the path of the Jack Russell terrier, which yapped angrily and chased him, though, surprisingly, it could not outrun him.

"Lunchbox! Where are you going? Come back here!" cried Nate, astounded at the hound's speed. *"Lunchbox!"*

He watched helplessly as Lunchbox disappeared past the trees at the other end of the park, then started to give chase.

After six blocks, Nate finally stopped running. His lungs burned; his hair was soaked with perspiration. Lunchbox was nowhere in sight. He stopped near the city hall and bent over to catch his breath. Maybe his dog had doubled back and was already headed home—probably to get another look at Dad's projects. Nate frowned at the coiled leash in his hand and turned around toward home.

The big building was dirty. Greasy metallic smells assaulted Lunchbox's nose as he sniffed the floor. He blinked in the dim light, going over the modifications in his head again as he looked at the machines. They would work beautifully, if only he had a way to manipulate them.

I wish I had tentacles, or . . . those things my boy has. Can't do anything with these clumsy feet, he thought.

He turned and trotted out, calculating as he went.

Nate decided to take a shortcut down Industrial Street. The sidewalk was cracked and overgrown in a lot of places. He wondered how many people had lost their jobs when the cannery folded. He gazed across the street at the old building. A high fence surrounded the plant. Tall weeds protruded from cracks in the parking lot, as well as along the perimeter of the fence.

The front gate of the building was bent, probably from an encounter with an inattentive truck driver, and though chained shut, left a gap at the bottom about eighteen inches wide. Lunchbox suddenly slipped out through the gap and greeted Nate with a nonchalant sniff, as if this meeting were entirely routine. Nate quickly snapped on the leash. "Don't you run off like that again! Bad dog!"

Lunchbox whimpered and meekly followed Nate home. Now what did I do? he wondered.

12

ate that evening, Lunchbox sat brooding in the darkened kitchen, his nose pointed at the door to the garage, his thoughts boring right through it.

There has to be a way. The tools and the technology are all available to me. He scratched at his ear with one of his back feet. *Maybe if I concentrate hard enough I can evolve something that works, like the Nizbliks on Blorfing Two. The Encyclopedia of Everything Else says they can do it overnight.* He squinted his eyes and lowered his head, letting the wrinkles fall forward along with his ears.

Come on, feet . . . I need appendages. Opposable digits would be nice. Come on, tail . . . if you can wag, maybe you can turn into a tentacle.

Nothing happened. Lunchbox realized, of course, that if he *had* managed to evolve overnight, there would have been a lot of explaining to do, and probably a trip to the vet or something. Explaining . . . if I could just explain it to somebody . . . if only I could make someone understand . . . someone I could trust . . .

Lunchbox opened his eyes and wagged his tail slightly as a wonderful idea formed in his mind.

Nate woke slowly, only slightly aware of the tugging at his covers. Not until a large tongue slurped across his face did he sit up. He reached for his glasses and looked at the clock.

"Lunchbox, it's three-thirty in the morning!" he hissed, flopping back onto the pillow.

"Hrrrrmmmmm," moaned Lunchbox. Impatiently, he hopped onto the bed beside Nate and used his teeth to pull the chain on the bedside lamp.

"What?" said Nate, squinting painfully.

"Mmmurf." Lunchbox leaped to the floor and headed for the door, where he stopped and turned around, softly *murf*ing again.

"Okay, I'm coming! I thought you went before bed-time!"

Lunchbox led him quietly down the hall, but instead of heading for the back door, he went into the den, where the computer screen cast a blue light around the room.

"Tell me you haven't been playing with Dad's computer again," whispered Nate. "You'll get me grounded for the whole summer!"

Lunchbox leaped onto the chair and pawed the mouse. The screen saver clicked off and a program window appeared. Nate looked at the toolbar heading. Even with all of Lunchbox's recent weirdness, what he saw still surprised him.

"You made a *PowerPoint* file?"

The first slide showed two funny-looking creatures, kind of like the mom and dad drawings Nate did when he was in preschool. These illustrations were lopsided circles with long wavy things that vaguely represented arms or something. One circle was larger than the other; both of them looked sort of like onions just pulled from the ground, but with round feet. Also, the onions were frowning. Or maybe they were squids—Nate really couldn't tell.

The next slide showed something rather lumpy and boxy suspended above a NASA photograph of Earth. On closer inspection, Nate could see a window in the lumpy-boxy thing. The two onion-squids waved from it.

"A spaceship!" said Nate excitedly.

Stay-sit. Why does he want me to "stay-sit"? thought Lunchbox. Sometimes this boy makes no sense at all. I'm already stay-sitting.

The third slide showed a photo of Lunchbox. It was

the same photo Nate's mom had used on the lost-dog flyer. Also on the screen were the two aliens again, waving their arm-things.

The fourth was again of Lunchbox, this time smaller, alongside what Nate recognized as one of his dad's drawings. A clip-art picture of a wrench and a hammer appeared, followed by a scan of Nate's third-grade picture, next to the tools.

The last slide showed the aliens. This time they were smiling.

Nate leaned back and tried to collect his thoughts.

"So, let me see if I understand this. . . . You need me to help you . . . build a *spaceship*?"

Again? Why does he keep saying "stay-sit"? thought Lunchbox.

"Wow, this is so cool!" Nate was thrilled to finally have another piece of the puzzle. Of course aliens had to be involved—ordinary people didn't leave weird radioactive things lying around in the woods for dogs to dig up.

"You must be . . . the Chosen One," said Nate. "Selected for first contact." This made sense, until he thought some more. "So why would they pick you instead of a human?"

He thought on this for a little longer. Of course they couldn't pick a human! Who could depend on one? A human would blab, or call the army and cause widespread

70

panic, and then there'd be real trouble. Who could they trust more than a loyal basset hound?

Nate hugged Lunchbox. "We're going to build a spaceship!"

Lunchbox shook his head. I AM "stay-sitting."

13

The rumbling in his belly was so loud Frazz could hardly hear himself groaning.

One *froonga* stick left. It was locked just across the cabin in a storage compartment. He trembled painfully. The creature down on the planet was still at least several days away from a solution, if any at all. Frazz again considered the possibility of sending Grunfloz to build the machine himself. Surely Grunfloz could handle those creatures, should they give him any trouble.

Then again, this planet was different. There weren't many planets that even Grunfloz feared to set foot on. His eyestalks followed the goo trail up the wall to the oozy thing's nest. Grunfloz had sloshed through the swamps of

Furporis Twelve for days, braving slime rains, strangling vines, large hungry reptiles, and exploding vapor pits to retrieve that disgusting specimen.

Once Grunfloz had even wrestled a Fribellian *kreekor*, just so he could recover a little jar of *droob* flies that had fallen out of his specimen bag and hit the creature's snout as it poked out of the steaming sand. The fang it left embedded in his upper right tentacle caused a festering rash that lasted for several months, but Grunfloz never once complained about it. He just added the fang to his trophy collection, hoping to tell the story to his future grand-Scwozzworts.

There were things on this planet far worse than Fribellian *kreekors*, however, and Grunfloz was probably right to avoid going to the surface. Frazz decided against ordering him to go. Not that ordering Grunfloz to do anything *worked*.

Frazz's eyestalks again leaned toward the compartment with the *froonga* locked in it. The lock had a timer and would only open at intervals that Frazz had programmed. He waited anxiously for the next opening. One bite, that's all he would take, then he'd put the *froonga* stick back and wait until the next time. After what seemed as long as they'd been out in space, the lock buzzed. Frazz lunged across the room and yanked the compartment open. With trembling tentacles he extracted the stick, measured carefully, and took a bite. *Ummmm.* He examined the location of the line he had scratched to see if any additional crumbs were still above it and therefore legal to eat in this session.

The temptation was almost overwhelming. Frazz found himself backing away from the compartment, toward his couch, holding the *froonga* in front of him as he tried to recalculate how long it would last if he just took one more half-nibble past the ration mark.

A dark glob of something-or-other plopped onto the stick in his tentacle. It dripped down the sides until it covered the remaining portions. In horror, he looked up

to see the oozy thing from Furporis Twelve making another exit from its nest.

"Aaaarrrrrrggh! I'm going to throw you out of the air lock!" he screamed. The oozy thing paid him little mind, still burbling happily as it slid down the wall and glooped its way to the door, which quickly slid open and allowed it to pass. Frazz flung the ruined food at the wall. "Come back here, you little fungus!" He ran after it, his tentacles flailing. The oozy thing slithered to the bridge and disappeared behind a bank of circuitry and plumbing.

Grunfloz sat glumly in front of the viewer. He lifted one eyestalk toward Frazz. "Now what?"

Frazz's words came in heaving gasps. "That . . . that *thing* . . . ruined my last *froonga* stick!" His head tendrils, eyestalks, and even his tentacles were bright orange.

"You had a *froonga* stick left? And you weren't planning to *share* it?" Grunfloz yanked open the lid to his own empty stash. "Some commander you are!"

"You ate it *all*?" asked Frazz incredulously. "You *flarmgrok*!"

"You helped," snarled Grunfloz.

"You *shared* it with me, remember?"

"But *you* were hiding one. Who's the real *flarmgrok* here?"

"Your stupid little friend down there is no closer to finishing the machine than it was four days ago!"

"It *will* finish the project," snapped Grunfloz.

"Not that we'll live to see it," said Frazz. "Why don't you go down there and finish it *yourself*?"

"And why don't *you* just stick your eyestalks down your throat and *swallow your head*?" Turning almost as orange as Frazz, Grunfloz whipped his tentacles forward, rolled him up in a ball, and threw him over the communications panel. Frazz landed with a splat on the oozy thing, which squealed and wriggled up the side. With fifteen years of repressed fury boiling in him, Frazz leaped back over the panel just as Grunfloz turned off the gravity generator. Spinning out of control, he hit his head on the high domed ceiling and bounced back toward the deck. Grunfloz launched himself and slammed into Frazz in midair, wrapping him in a full-body tackle that sent them both bouncing around the dome in an orange and green tangle. Frazz managed to work an eyestalk loose, trying to figure out which way was up. Below them, the oozy thing snagged onto the communications panel, where it formed little appendages that poked at various switches on the console.

"Grnfloph! Ith trinda henda meffage!" said Frazz through a mouthful of Grunfloz's tentacle. Grunfloz growled and squeezed harder.

"Grmflovh! Owww!" Frazz worked the tip of his tentacle until he managed to wrap it around one of

Grunfloz's eyestalks and yanked with all his might, forcing him to look toward the deck.

"Graarrgh!" roared Grunfloz, loosening his grip slightly.

"It's trying to send a message!" gasped Frazz, finally able to move his tongue. Grunfloz continued bellowing. Frazz grabbed the other eyestalk and twisted it next to the first one. "Look at the oozy thing!"

Grunfloz yanked his eyestalks out of Frazz's grip and sent him spinning back toward the ceiling. Looping a tentacle down around the gravity switch, he flipped it on, landing not quite gently on the deck across from the communications panel. Frazz fell screaming from the dome, landing even less gently on the deck near his command couch. The oozy thing busied itself with punching buttons and switches, extending so many appendages at once that it looked like a spiny ballfish from the moons of *Oogachaka*. Grunfloz checked the readout. It *was* trying to send a message! The display on the screen highlighted a distant sector of space near the edge of the solar system.

"Ooze! Get off of there!" he barked. The oozy thing reblobbed itself and squished away in surprise.

"Bbbbblorp?"

Grunfloz rubbed his eyestalks where Frazz had twisted them. He spoke a little more gently, but still with irritation in his voice. "Go on, Ooze. Go back to your nest. Go on. Shoo!"

Frazz pulled himself up to his command couch and slumped painfully. "You show more respect to that blob than you've ever shown to me."

"Actually," said Grunfloz, "I've *never* respected you."

"And I don't suppose you're going to start now," sighed Frazz.

"No. Probably not."

14

When Nate awoke the next morning, Lunchbox was gone. He heard his father shouting and stumbled into the hall to hear what the commotion was about.

"Call the police, Connie! Someone's stolen my inventions!"

Nate dashed to the garage. The door was wide open and all of the machines were missing. Nate had a sudden sickly feeling.

"I *know* I locked the garage!" said Mr. Parker.

Mrs. Parker appeared from the kitchen, telephone in hand.

"Is anything else missing?"

Mr. Parker, even more agitated, scanned the garage quickly. "I don't think so—wait—my tools! They're all gone!"

Lunchbox! thought Nate. He's really going to get me in trouble now.

The police were checking out the crime scene and talking with Mr. Parker when Lunchbox ambled up the driveway, looking extremely pleased with himself. He ignored the people in the garage and trotted over to Nate's bicycle, where he woofed impatiently. Seeing that the adults were all busy, Nate quickly hopped on the bicycle. Lunchbox took off running at lightning speed with the boy in pursuit. Nate was only mildly surprised when they turned on Industrial Street. With the cannery closed, it was easy to lock his bike to the fence and slip through the gap in the gate unseen. They hurried to the side entrance by the loading dock, where all of Mr. Parker's inventions and tools were, as well as Nate's wagon. Using the wagon, they hauled everything in, one piece at a time.

"Dad's gonna kill us if he ever finds out," said Nate. "This thing better work!"

Lunchbox bounded up the steps and through the open door; Nate stopped and peered nervously inside. About half a dozen long, cylindrical pressure cookers sat idly among a tangle of conveyor belts and scaffolding. The cookers—or *retorts*—that was the term he'd heard used once—were about twenty feet long and five or six feet high, with heavy iron hatches. A couple of them were open, revealing large steel baskets on wheels. Lunchbox barked encouragingly, having quickly made an inspection lap around the cannery floor.

It took the better part of the morning for Nate to make sense of Lunchbox's drawings and to figure out which piece of what machine should go where. Pieces of machinery that were never originally meant to go together were joined under Lunchbox's direction. Nate found the work harder than anything he'd ever done. Many of the bolts were stuck or rusted, requiring every ounce of his strength to loosen.

At the same time, it was thrilling. Here he was, someplace where he had no business being, doing something that was probably illegal, all for the advancement of science. The world would soon be thanking them for their efforts. Nate and Lunchbox, Galactic Ambassadors!

They worked continuously for several days. Nate had great difficulty getting Lunchbox to take breaks, and more difficulty making him understand when it was time to go home.

Nothing was as difficult as explaining to his parents why he came home so greasy and grimy every day, however.

"I'm helping Connor Franklin build a go-cart," he

said at the dinner table. He hated to lie, but he told himself he'd be able to make it all clear to them when the project was finished. Once the aliens were contacted and dialogue was begun, it would usher in world peace, as the nations of Earth united to learn from an advanced civilization—even if they did look like onions, or squids.

Mr. Parker glumly looked at Nate, who was working on his third helping of tuna casserole. A small glob of cheese sauce remained on his plate where the broccoli had been.

"That must be some go-cart you're building, Son."

"Oh-h-h-h yeah," said Nate.

"I didn't know you liked broccoli."

"Calcium for strong bones and teeth, and a natural painkiller. Vitamin A for eyesight. Antioxidants for the immune system. I have to be really healthy if I'm going to be an astronaut."

"Uh . . . yeah, I guess you're right," said Mr. Parker. "An astronaut . . ."

"When I grow up," added Nate quickly. "I mean, it's not like I'm going into space *next week*, you know."

"That's good news," said his mother. "Then Daddy would have to mow the lawn." She gave her husband one of those "neener-neener" looks.

Mr. Parker frowned and stared at the wall. Nate knew he was thinking about his lost inventions.

"Keep trying, Dad. You'll succeed sooner or later."

"I'd love to agree with you, Son, but I've lost my youthful idealism. Now, if you two will excuse me, I've got to go take care of some *paying* work." Mr. Parker headed for the den, grumbling.

"What's 'useful idealism'?" Nate asked his mother.

She sighed wearily. "Something I don't ever want you to lose."

15

"**F**razz! Open up!" Grunfloz pounded on the hatch to Frazz's quarters. "They're building it!"

The hatch hissed open to reveal a very disheveled Frazz. His head tendrils were swollen and lumpy, and his lids clamped around his eyes as if trying to keep them from falling off their stalks.

"Who's 'they'?" he mumbled.

"The creature and its keeper! They're building the *froonga* machine!"

"Lovely. Can I go back to dying now?"

Grunfloz shook him with both tentacles. "Come on, hurry!" Grunfloz half-dragged Frazz to the bridge.

"It won't be long now," said Grunfloz. "We're going to have *froonga* soon! Just another day or two."

"*Froonga*," rasped Frazz. "I almost can't remember what it tastes like."

Looking at playbacks of the creature's work, he felt no comfort. To him, it was a jumbled mass of odd machine parts that didn't resemble the *froonga* machines back home at all. And the creatures building it—they were too alien, too ugly, too stupid. In spite of the fact that one of them had the entire Scwozzwort engineering library dumped into its head, Frazz could not ignore feelings of impending disaster.

"It's time to send the *plookie* regulator," said Grunfloz.

That was it, Frazz realized. Stupid creatures, careless Grunfloz, a terrible destructive force—the disaster formula looked pretty much complete.

The finished contraption was a sight to behold. A bunch of scrambled machine parts from the cannery had been arranged in a circular pattern. Metal arms extended at regular intervals, wrapped in wire. The whole thing could have resembled a spaceship if one squinted and used a lot of imagination. In the center they had mounted the hot water heater/laundry sterilizer. Nate wasn't sure if this was supposed to be a warp core or if it was the passenger capsule—it didn't look big enough to fit a boy and a basset in there together. Maybe it would just generate a force field bubble around them and give them an unobstructed view of the universe as they hurtled through it.

After Nate had bolted on the last piece of equipment, Lunchbox stared intently at the machine for several minutes. Nate stood beside him, feeling as proud as he was confused. A sudden flash of light on the loading dock outside startled him. Lunchbox trotted to the dock and returned with a strange-looking disk in his mouth. It resembled a large Frisbee, but it was thicker in the middle, with greenish glowing spots around its edges.

"Where did that come from?" asked Nate. "I don't remember Dad having that!"

Lunchbox carried the disk up the metal steps to the top of the machine. He inserted it onto four conduits bent at right angles, which fit exactly into ports spaced evenly on the bottom of it. He howled triumphantly.

"Arrooooooo!"

Nate's excitement was at fever pitch. "So how do we test it? We're going to test it now, right?"

Lunchbox hopped down from the machine and headed for the door.

"Where are you going? Lunchbox! Wait for me!" Nate chased after him. Lunchbox stopped to grab the wagon by its handle and bounced it down the steps by the dock.

"Hey! Be careful with that, it's mine!" shouted Nate. Lunchbox stopped at the gap in the gate. The wagon wouldn't fit until they turned it on its side and shoved it through. Lunchbox took off running. Nate grabbed the wagon and gave chase. It rattled and bounced on the cracks in the sidewalk. On the next block, Lunchbox ducked into the alley. When Nate finally caught up, sweating and puffing, Lunchbox was barking at a closed Dumpster behind the local diner.

"What?" wheezed Nate. Lunchbox grew more agitated. Nate cautiously climbed onto an empty crate and lifted the Dumpster's lid. "Ewww, gross!" The smell of rotting food made him gag.

Lunchbox whined impatiently.

"What, you want me to put garbage in my wagon? Are you nuts?"

"Hrrrrmmmmmmmm!"

"Okay, but I don't see what this has to do with—*oof*—building a spaceship!" Nate hauled out two smelly bags and plopped them onto the wagon. "Is that enough?"

Lunchbox barked for more. Nate groaned and climbed back into the Dumpster to retrieve another bag, which he balanced on the others.

"There's no more room!" He felt like throwing up. A swarm of flies protested as he climbed back out. His clothes, already stained with industrial grime, were now soaked with whatever had leaked out of the bags.

"I hope you're happy now. I smell like death!"

Lunchbox wagged his tail as they made their way back to the cannery. The flies followed, buzzing around their heads. Nate slapped at his ears until they rang.

Getting the garbage bags through the gate was no easy task. Nate had to stand in the rickety wagon and try to heave them over the high fence, but they splattered onto the pavement and split open, making an even bigger mess. Eventually he just shoved the empty wagon sideways through the gate and began passing piles of garbage through the gap with his bare hands. Lunchbox picked up the mess in his mouth and dropped it into the wagon. Nate gagged and choked but finally got the last of the slimy mass of lettuce, old chicken bones, mustard, napkins, and things he would not even try to identify into the wagon.

They hauled the reeking load up the steps, with Lunchbox pulling on the handle and Nate pushing from behind, which caused some of the glop-mountain to fall on him as they worked.

Finally the wagon was parked at the edge of the machine. With his fat paw Lunchbox switched on the power and the machine began humming, clacking, whirring, and vibrating. The disk at the top glowed brightly. Bolts of energy arced between the wire-wrapped arms. Without hesitation, Lunchbox began flinging garbage into the snowblower scoop that protruded from one side.

As astonishing as everything to this point had been, Nate could not believe what he was seeing. A spaceship that ran on garbage—the world was going to be in for some real surprises! He vigorously pitched in, ignoring the smell, until they had emptied the wagonload into the machine.

The machine thrummed and made grinding noises; the water heater glowed with a greenish white light.

"It's working! It's working!" Nate cheered. Lunchbox barked excitedly.

A hatch at the other end hissed open, ejecting several steaming green bricks onto a conveyor belt. Before Nate could think about what they were for, Lunchbox bounded to the end of the machine and began eating the bricks, chomping and snarfing like a starving wolf with a fresh kill.

Nate's jaw flopped open. "Lunchbox! You . . . I . . . I lied to my parents! I worked like a dog! I climbed into a Dumpster and got totally gross and dirty! You put me through all of this . . . just so you could EAT GARBAGE?"

16

Frazz twiddled his tentacles nervously. The creature had devoured the first batch.

"What if it doesn't want to share? What if it just eats everything?"

"Then you starve and I finally get some peace and quiet," growled Grunfloz.

Frazz was too weak to reply. They sat silently, the noises from their empty stomachs providing all the conversation necessary. They watched as the creature placed block after block into the little cart, until it was piled higher than it could reach. Occasionally the creature turned its attention to the scrawny little biped that seemed to be sulking instead of helping.

"Yuck, what a monster," mumbled Frazz.

"Look, it's moving the cart!" said Grunfloz. "It's on the platform!" He quickly activated the capture beam. "Here it comes!"

The Scwozzworts raced to the capture bay. Grunfloz yanked the hatch open. There sat the little wheeled cart with its steaming load of green bricks. Frazz bobbed his eyestalks into the hatchway to look. Grunfloz shoved him out of the way and lumbered inside. Frazz picked himself up and followed.

"Has it been decontaminated?" asked Frazz. "This *is* alien *froonga*, you know."

"Why don't you give it the first taste?" Grunfloz pointed at the samples.

"Me? Why me?"

"Because you're the captain."

"Oh, NOW I'm the captain," Frazz snapped.

"Just *taste* it!" roared Grunfloz.

Frazz gingerly touched the stack with his trembling tentacle, making sure there were no organisms waiting to attack him. He hefted one of the bricks and examined it.

"*Froonga* isn't supposed to look like that," he said. "It always comes in sticks!"

"So what! Taste it!"

Frazz noted a few tooth marks.

"It drooled on it!"

"It drools on everything! *Taste it!*"

"All right, I'm tasting, I'm tasting!" Frazz broke off a small corner and put it cautiously in his mouth.

"Well?"

Frazz rolled the sample around on his tongue and swallowed slowly.

Grunfloz glared at him. "Well? How is it?"

Frazz made a sour face. "It tastes like *rurfroo*."

"*Rurfroo?*" Grunfloz snatched a brick from the stack and stuck the whole thing in his mouth, chewing vigorously. He stared at Frazz in disbelief.

"You're *furmnorkle*! This is delicious!" shouted Grunfloz, showering crumbs on the deck. Frazz broke into raucous laughter.

"It's better than delicious! It's the best *froonga* I've ever tasted!" said Frazz gleefully. "Fooled you!" He crammed the remainder of the brick into his mouth and chewed as disgustingly as Grunfloz.

"*Froongaaaaaaaa!*" they shouted together, and began a furious *froonga* feeding frenzy that didn't end until the cart was empty.

Nate rubbed his eyes. When he was able to focus, he saw Lunchbox sitting at the edge of the dock, gazing into the sky.

"What happened to the wagon?"

Lunchbox trotted back into the warehouse and began sniffing around the machine for any leftover garbage. The bright light flashed again.

Nate turned around. His wagon was back, empty, looking slightly battered and grimy. Suddenly feeling weak in the knees, he sat down and drew a deep breath.

"Lunchbox, this is really weirding me out."

17

"**N**ate, did you take the garbage out?"

"Yeah." Nate picked absently at his breakfast.

Mrs. Parker shrugged. "Hmm. I didn't hear the truck, but it's gone already."

"I'm not surprised," mumbled Nate. He took his hand off the spoon and watched his cereal get soggier.

"Something wrong?" his mother asked. "You don't seem to be in such a hurry today."

"Just tired, that's all." He didn't tell her that Lunchbox had kept him up half the night with another slide show. From what he'd been able to determine from the crude pictures, the glowing Frisbee-looking thing was important to making the garbage machine work right. He wasn't sure

95

what the picture of Earth breaking into pieces meant—either the aliens would destroy the world if he and Lunchbox messed up, or Lunchbox wasn't very good with clip art.

"How's the go-cart coming along?" asked his father.

"It didn't work," said Nate dejectedly. "It isn't going anywhere."

"Oh. That's too bad," said Mr. Parker. He continued eating, staring at the wall in a sort of half-focused way. He hadn't smiled much at all since the burglary.

Mrs. Parker tried to brighten things up. "Has anyone noticed how frisky Lunchbox has been? I've never seen him with so much energy!"

"Too bad we can't bottle it and sell it," said Mr. Parker. "Then we could all *enjoy* working like dogs."

"Lunchbox has some new friends," said Nate. "I don't think he'll stay home much now."

Mr. Parker looked at his watch and groaned to himself. "Well, back to the salt mines." He dragged himself up and lifted his briefcase as if it weighed sixty pounds. "Durwood's excited about a new stupid idea."

"Don't give up," said Mrs. Parker. "I still think you're too brilliant for him." She pecked him on the cheek as he opened the front door. The sound of the garbage truck stopping pierced the air.

"That's odd," she said. "Nate, are you *sure* you took the trash out?"

"Yes, I did."

"I wonder where it went. Everyone's trash is still at the curb except ours . . . and Mrs. Giggelberger's."

"No clue," said Nate. *Lunchbox.* He pushed the unfinished bowl away, grabbed his backpack, and went out to his bike on the porch.

His mother stuck her head out of the front door. "Be home for lunch. And *please* don't get so filthy this time! I can't get that grease out of your clothes."

When Nate got to the cannery, he found Lunchbox at the gate with the wagon. It was piled high with several bags of garbage. The dog held a metal file between his teeth and was furiously sawing away at the chain-link fence. Three links were already severed. Metal fragments coated his jowls and covered the sidewalk under the gate, mixed in with little puddles of drool.

"Lunchbox! You can't do that!"

Lunchbox growled and kept working the file. His whole body convulsed with the effort; his ears flapped out of control as he moved his head back and forth. The fourth link popped. He dropped the file with a clang and panted for a moment, then wriggled through the opening and peeled the fence back with his teeth, making a hole big enough to get the garbage bags through.

Nate looked around nervously. "What if someone sees us?"

Lunchbox ignored him and dragged a bag through the opening, then came out to retrieve the next one.

Nate heard the roar of a diesel engine down the street.

"Someone's coming!" He stood frozen for a minute, trying to figure out what to do. Quickly he shoved two more bags into the opening, then crammed the wagon through. "Hurry!" He flung the bags back into the wagon and began wheeling it toward the loading dock. One bag remained on the sidewalk. As Lunchbox headed out to get it, the garbage truck braked with a deafening squeal. A man hopped off the rear platform while it was still moving, grabbed the bag, flung it into the compactor, and climbed back onto his perch. The truck accelerated up the street.

Lunchbox chased after it, bellowing angrily. "*Barrrooooo!*"

Nate let go of the wagon and ran back to the gate.

"Lunchbox! No!" He scrambled through the hole, leaped onto his bike, and pumped hard to catch up. Lunchbox chased the truck around the corner onto Main Street. Nate heard the garbagemen laughing as he got closer.

"Oh, no!" said Nate. As they neared Thornhill Enterprises, he saw his father preparing to cross the street. Mr. Parker paused to let the truck pass, then stepped into the street and nearly tripped over Lunchbox, who ignored him and continued chasing and barking. Nate whizzed past his surprised father, quickly blurting out, "Hi, Dad—bye, Dad!" He pumped harder, hearing the angry voice fade behind him.

"Nate! Get out of the street! *Naaaaaate . . .*"

At the next stop sign, the truck's brakes screeched again, like fingernails on a giant chalkboard. Lunchbox closed the gap between them and bounded into the truck, barking and snarling so viciously that the men leaped off and backed away in fear. Lunchbox seized a garbage bag in his teeth and jumped out, dragging it onto the pavement. It was only a few seconds before it ripped and spread its contents all over the street. Lunchbox continued running for a few feet with the empty bag before he stopped and surveyed the mess.

Nate pulled up behind him and snatched him by the scruff of his neck. "Bad dog!"

The garbagemen cursed and climbed back onto the platform, leaving Nate to clean up the street by himself.

"Hey, kid, tie up that dog, will ya?" shouted one of them as the truck continued on its route.

"Sorry about that!" shouted Nate through a cloud of diesel exhaust.

He tugged hard on Lunchbox. "Will you stop all this weird stuff? You're gonna get me arrested!" He pulled the torn bag from the dog's mouth and started picking up the garbage, wrapping the mess in the plastic as best he could, but the bag was too mangled to be of much use. Holding the reeking bundle at arm's length, he searched in vain for a trash can or Dumpster. Finally he dropped it in some tall grass near the stop sign and hoped he wasn't seen littering. Lunchbox whined in protest.

"No, we're just going to leave it!" snapped Nate. "Come on, let's go!" He tugged at the dog again. Lunchbox resisted at first but finally moaned and plodded behind the bicycle as Nate walked it along the sidewalk. He gradually perked up as they got closer to the cannery. By the time they reached the gate, Lunchbox's tail was wagging vigorously and he was ready to work again.

Nate froze. The gate was unlocked and wide open.

18

Two fancy cars and a garbage truck sat on the cracked asphalt outside of the building. Nate recognized one car as Mayor Thornhill's; the truck was from Purvis Sanitation. It was identical to the one Lunchbox had chased.

At the sight of the garbage truck, Lunchbox growled.

"No, Lunchbox!" hissed Nate. "Be quiet!" He moved slowly to the edge of the loading dock and ducked down behind it. Lunchbox followed, and the two of them huddled there for a moment. Nate heard voices echoing across the concrete floor, and peered up over the dock to see who was talking.

Durwood Thornhill conversed with a man in an expensive suit. Nearby stood Leland Purvis, wearing his garbageman coveralls. The man in the suit gestured and pointed around the building as he talked. Mayor Thornhill nodded from time to time, asking questions. Mr. Purvis wandered around examining the machinery. His eyes fell on Lunchbox's creation.

"Yo, lookit this! Whaddaya think this thing's for?"

Mayor Thornhill looked annoyed. The well-dressed man shrugged.

"I don't know what all these machines do, I just handled the bankruptcy for the cannery. I'm sure they're all identified in my files."

Nate decided the man was a lawyer or something.

Lunchbox, unable to see what was going on, became agitated. As the men turned in his direction again, Nate ducked down and put a hand on Lunchbox's back to calm him, though he could feel his own heart pounding in his ears. Apparently the mayor was planning to buy the property. Nate quickly tried to calculate the chain of events this might trigger. All of the machines would be sold or junked, including Lunchbox's marvelous creation. The aliens would definitely be upset. Mayor Thornhill's voice brought Nate back to the moment.

"We'll work out a bid and meet after the Fourth."

"Fair enough," said the lawyer.

Nate stole another glance over at the platform. He saw the mayor and the lawyer shaking hands while Purvis climbed around the garbage machine, jiggling various parts. Lunchbox growled. Nate clamped a hand around the hound's muzzle and grabbed his scruff with the other one, spinning him around away from the corner of the platform. He ducked down again as the men exited through the side door. He could hear the footsteps coming very close to the corner of the dock. Nate noticed then that Lunchbox's tail was sticking out in their path. He held his breath, and nearly exploded when the mayor's foot came within an inch of it.

"Lots of work to do on this—see if they'll knock another fifty grand off their price," said Mayor Thornhill.

Nate could feel himself starting to black out but still held his breath and held on tightly to Lunchbox. He didn't exhale until the group turned and walked toward the parking lot in front.

"I can't guarantee anything," said the lawyer. "Be sure and put the lock on the gate—it looks like kids have been playing in here."

"Yes, of course." Mayor Thornhill smiled cheerily as the lawyer got into his car. As soon as the car left the parking lot, he turned and snapped at Purvis.

"Leland! You wanna move this heap so I can get my car out?"

"That ain't no heap! That's the best truck I got!"

"You haven't gotten those new trucks yet?"

"I couldn't get the loan, *yer honor*. You didn't come through like you promised." Purvis's angry voice changed to a pleading tone. "That extra 2½ percent is killin' me. And my kid's got a birthday comin' up."

The mayor shrugged. "Looks like you're going to be moonlighting," he said smugly.

"Whaddaya mean?"

Thornhill gestured at the building. "I have a whole cannery full of machinery that's been sitting for years. I want you and your goons to get it all cleaned up and running."

"But you ain't even bought this place yet!"

Thornhill smiled and handed him a key. "It's just a formality. That lawyer's got no reason to set foot here again—we'll get all the papers signed and that'll be it."

"I ain't got time to clean this place up! I got a business to run!"

"You know, there *is* that other bid that the city council hasn't seen yet."

Purvis cursed under his breath. "I shoulda known this deal wasn't as sweet as you painted it."

"Move your truck, I've got a lot of work to do . . . and so do you. Have it done by the time the papers are signed."

Purvis climbed into the cab of the garbage truck and slammed the door. The sound of the engine's metallic gargling drowned out his swearing.

"Wait! You forgot this!" Mayor Thornhill grabbed Nate's wagon full of garbage bags and tossed it into the back of the truck. Purvis activated the compactor. Nate's wagon crumpled with a sickening crunch and disappeared. Lunchbox snarled angrily as Purvis drove off.

Thornhill started his car and pulled out, stopping to lock the gate behind him, and frowned at the hole that Lunchbox had cut in it. He glanced curiously at Nate's bicycle by the fence, and drove off with his cell phone to his ear.

Nate shook his head wearily. "We're in big doo-doo now, Lunchbox."

19

There was only enough garbage left to make three more bricks. Nate allowed Lunchbox to eat one, but wrapped the remaining two in plastic and stuffed them in his backpack.

They arrived home after five. He had forgotten all about going home for lunch. Between chasing garbage trucks, eavesdropping on shady business deals, crawling through Dumpsters, and making alien food, he'd forgotten to eat. He braced himself for another lecture, but his mother was too preoccupied to nag him about being gone all day. His father sat in his chair with a stack of papers in his lap, scowling as he scanned them one by one.

"Durwood's trying to kill me," he groaned. "I'll be up every night and all weekend trying to finish this."

"It's a holiday weekend coming up," said Mrs. Parker. "Surely he'll let you take some time off."

"He wants all of this stuff ready before the Fourth," said Mr. Parker.

"What *is* that?" Mrs. Parker eyed the stack of papers.

"His latest dumb idea. He's buying the old cannery and says he'll put the whole town back to work."

"But?"

"But I know Durwood. He wants me to find the market value of every piece of equipment in that plant so he can sell it after the election. He knows the cannery will never re-open. He just wants the property so Pete Carson doesn't get it."

"Dad, what does Mr. Carson do?" asked Nate.

"He's on the city council, and he's also running for mayor."

"No, I mean, what does he do for a living? What's his job?"

"He's an investor, mostly in real estate and insurance."

"Why didn't you go to him with your ideas?"

Mr. Parker drew a deep breath again. "Well, that should be obvious, Son. It's called 'fraternizing with the enemy.'"

"But he's not *your* enemy. He's the *mayor's* enemy."

"It's complicated, Nate. Let's just say I don't need Mayor Thornhill as my enemy, too, and leave it at that."

"Sounds like he already is," said Mrs. Parker, rising from her chair to return to the kitchen. "You just won't deal with it." Mr. Parker started to open his mouth, but Nate interrupted.

"Dad? Why don't you ask Mr. Carson for a job?"

Mr. Parker sighed. "He pretty much stays with his crowd from the Dog & Gun Club."

"The what?"

"A bunch of rich guys who get together at the lodge in Hooverton on weekends with their hunting dogs and try to impress one another."

Nate's face brightened. "Mr. Carson has dogs?"

"Prize-winners, I'm told. But . . ."

"How many dogs does he have?"

"Nate, what does this have to do with anything?"

"Nothing. Just curious."

"Well, I don't know. There's a lot about Mr. Carson I don't know. In fact, I hardly know *anything* about him except what Mr. Thornhill tells me, and I have to—oh, never mind." Mr. Parker took his glasses off and rubbed between his eyes. "Where was I, Connie?"

"Apparently going nowhere," said Mrs. Parker curtly.

Nate excused himself and led Lunchbox to his room. After thinking carefully for several minutes, he put his arm around the dog and whispered in his ear.

"Lunchbox, we have to keep Mayor Thornhill from buying the cannery."

20

"That was the best *froonga* binge ever! I feel like my old self again." Grunfloz patted his belly and belched vigorously.

Frazz leaned back, completely blissed out. "You can say that again."

"Brrraaaaaahp!" repeated Grunfloz. "It sure beat *your* expectations, didn't it? I always knew it would work." He smacked his lips. "And did it ever!"

"You're right," said Frazz. He pointed a tentacle at him. "Lowly Enlisted Scwozzwort Third Class Grunfloz, I hereby refer you for a commendation."

"I don't want a medal, *sir*, just an apology."

"Fine. I apologize . . . um . . . for whatever it was."

"For doubting me."

"For doubting you." Frazz waved a tentacle in the air, as if conducting an imaginary orchestra on the ceiling.

"And the creature," Grunfloz insisted.

"And the creature," repeated Frazz.

"Apology accepted." Grunfloz pulled himself upright in his control couch. "Let's see how the next batch is doing."

"The next batch!" Frazz felt giddy.

Grunfloz switched on the viewer and began replaying highlights from the last several hours. He let out a small grunt and watched in silence for several minutes. Switching to the long-range scanners, he focused on the building that housed the *froonga* machine.

Frazz remained on his back, but turned his eyestalks toward Grunfloz.

"Well, how's it coming?"

Grunfloz didn't answer. Frazz felt the giddiness dissipate quickly. He could see a hint of orange at the base of Grunfloz's head tendrils.

"Well?" said Frazz nervously.

Grunfloz sat back and let out a long sigh.

"We have a problem."

"A problem!" Frazz leaped to his feet. "What kind of problem?"

"Intruders."

Lunchbox sprinted through the darkened streets. The message from the big smelly animal reverberated in his brain. *Intruders.*

His ears streamed out behind his head as he put on more speed, turning the corner so quickly that his back feet skidded on the sand-covered pavement. With graceful precision he aimed for the gate and accelerated.

Clannng!

Lunchbox bounced off of the gate like a volleyball off of a net. Bright lights popped and swirled in his head. He crumpled on the concrete and lay still for several minutes.

Slowly, he got up. His snout throbbed and a stinging pain persisted on his forehead, as if it had been scraped badly. He stared at the gate where he had aimed his body.

Some *gargafron* repaired the gate, he fumed. He sniffed along the fence for another entrance. Several yards past the gate, the pavement ended, giving way to dry weeds and hard dirt. Lunchbox began digging furiously.

"What happened?" shouted Frazz, almost yanking Grunfloz's head tendrils off.

Grunfloz swatted Frazz's tentacle away. "We've lost the link! No vital signs, no picture!" He quickly replayed the sequence.

"The stupid thing ran into the fence!" blurted Frazz. "It's probably killed itself!"

Grunfloz switched to the overhead viewer and began scanning the area around the *froonga* plant for life-forms.

"It's hard to see," he said. "Looks like maybe four or five of those bipeds moving in and out near the loading platform, but—wait—look! Right there!" Grunfloz pointed to a corner of the screen and increased the magnification. A small dark shape was wriggling under the barrier.

"It's still alive!" cried Frazz.

"Yes, but I think it's lost the scanner."

"We . . . we could always pick it up again, couldn't

112

we?" Frazz shuddered at the thought of letting that thing back on the ship.

"Maybe later—there isn't time to worry about it now. It's got to protect the *froonga* machine!"

"We won't be able to see what's going on inside," said Frazz. "What if they kill it?" His head tendrils glowed bright orange.

Grunfloz scrunched his mouth up and thought for a moment. "If anything happens to the creature," he said, pausing to get a deep breath, "one of us will have to go down there."

21

It was the second day of July. Though still before noon, it was too hot to be outside one more minute, especially since Nate was wearing his best shirt and a tie. He chained his bike in front of Carson Investments. Taking a deep breath, he smoothed his wet hair and slowly ventured up the steps.

Lunchbox inspected the *froonga* machine carefully. Puddles of water lingered in low spots on the floor. It had been fun to watch the intruders run away, though turning off the water valve had not been as easy as turning it on.

The machine had endured the incident well. It was ready for more production.

Lunchbox cocked his ears at a familiar rumbling out in the street. Another one of those garbage-gathering vehicles! He wagged his tail eagerly.

This time you're not getting away.

Nate carefully unzipped his backpack and placed two greenish bricks on the elegant desk. Mr. Carson wrinkled his nose, as if Nate had just plopped a pair of fresh cow pies on the polished hardwood.

"What did you call this again?"

"Parker's Power Pooch Pellets. It's my dad's own formula," said Nate, trying not to sound nervous.

Mr. Carson raised his silver eyebrows. "And you say your dog loves this?"

"Yes, sir."

"Well, what's in it?"

"Umm . . . it's full of . . . *ingredients*. Vitamins—and a whole lot of other stuff."

"I'd like a little more proof," he said politely, but firmly. "I don't just throw money down on business ideas without something more solid to go on."

Nate bit his lip. The room grew very quiet. He could hear the noise from the street below. A garbage truck rumbled by, its engine roaring at full throttle.

Full throttle! Nate jumped up and ran to the window.

"Mr. Carson, there's your proof right there!" Mr. Carson moved to the window in time to see a basset hound sprint past at greyhound speed, closing in on the garbage truck like a floppy-eared cruise missile.

Mr. Carson's astonished eyes followed the dog until he was out of view.

"Quite a presentation, Mr. Parker. Your dog has great timing." He turned and faced Nate, leaned against the window, and folded his arms. "So what do you want me to do?"

"Feed those samples to your hunting dogs," said Nate, feeling a little bolder. "Give it to the oldest and weakest ones, and see what happens."

"Agreed. And?"

"And if it works, you'll help us buy the cannery before the fifth of July."

"That's a bit of a leap, isn't it? Isn't your father's boss trying to buy it?"

"It's all politics, sir. My dad said so."

"He did, hmm?"

"Here's my dad's business card," said Nate. "It's got his e-mail address on it."

Mr. Carson smiled as he took the card. "Nate, thank you for a very professional presentation." He shook Nate's hand firmly. "Your father must be a pretty smart man."

"That's what we keep trying to tell him," said Nate.

Lunchbox ran alongside the garbage-gatherer, barking furiously. The men on the back yelled and threw things at him, but he focused on the front of the vehicle. Suddenly a car appeared in his path, making a squealing sound as it tried to stop. With a burst of extra speed, Lunchbox leaped onto the car's hood and sprang into the air, making a perfect landing inside the open window of the garbage-gatherer as it rounded a curve in the road.

The men on the back fell off as their vehicle swerved. Lunchbox barked his loudest, frothiest barks right in the face of the driver, who jumped out immediately and rolled into the ditch with the other two. As the careening garbage-gatherer began picking up speed downhill, Lunchbox hurriedly surveyed the controls and came to a quick conclusion:

I have no idea how to drive this thing.

22

"Increase the power!" shouted Grunfloz.

Frazz stared helplessly at the array of switches and levers on the console. "Which one?"

"That one! Now!" Grunfloz waved a tentacle at the largest lever. "Pull it down all the way!"

Frazz looped both tentacles and tugged, practically hanging on it before it finally budged. The lights in the cabin dimmed. The whine of the ship's engines grew louder and the vibrations increased under his feet. Warning lights flashed and the emergency honker blared.

"I think it's overheating!" cried Frazz. "Are you sure you know what you're doing?"

"I'm saving the creature's life—and our *froonga*!" Grunfloz aimed the capture beam graphic until it was directly over the speeding garbage-gatherer. "I need the extra power to lift that thing!"

"If you blow up the engines, we'll be marooned here forever!"

"That's right!" shouted Grunfloz. "Marooned without *froonga*!" He watched the power gauge turn bright purple. Stray currents arced across the control panel; Frazz leaped back as one of the bolts stung his tentacle.

"Owww!"

"Steady—steeeeady—*got it!*" The engines bogged down with a strained grinding sound. The lights in the cabin grew even dimmer. The *Urplung Greebly* shuddered as the extra weight threatened to yank it from its orbit. "Hold on, just a few more seconds!" Grunfloz fumbled in the darkness to set the delivery coordinates. The garbage-gatherer dangled in the capture beam's grip high above the planet's surface, like a *droob* fly hanging from the tongue of a *snarzal* newt, except that in this case, the *droob* fly was massive enough to rip the *snarzal* newt's tongue out.

"Decrease the power slowly," barked Grunfloz. "We want to set it down gently!"

Frazz looped his tentacles under the green lever and strained. It was just as hard to push up as it had been to pull down, having never been moved from its default setting for the length of their voyage. Frazz hammered repeatedly to get it to budge.

"Keep it steady! Don't jerk it!" Grunfloz aimed the beam near the big building that housed the *froonga* machine. "Now—cut to three quarters—two thirds—hold on, not so fast!"

Smoke began billowing from the power grid.

"Ugh, that stinks!" Frazz coughed.

"We're losing it!" cried Grunfloz. "Still too high!" His tentacles flew over the controls as he attempted to adjust the remaining circuits.

Frazz continued to slowly force the lever. The engine's pitch dropped in response. Grunfloz tried to balance the garbage-gatherer's descent by tightening the containment beam, but the vehicle began to lean on its side.

"It's still too high above the surface! We're losing it! Increase the power again!"

"Make up your mind!" screamed Frazz. He began pulling on the lever, which suddenly refused to budge at all. He put both feet on the control panel and strained against it. "It's stuck!"

"Pull harder!" Grunfloz increased the magnification, zooming in on the vehicle's cabin. He could see the creature sticking its head out the window, its earflaps flying in the wind. The garbage-gatherer began falling as the capture beam became too weak to hold it. Frazz took a deep breath, wrapped his tentacles more tightly around the lever, tightened every muscle in his body, and screamed with the effort.

"Eeeeyaaaaaagh!" Suddenly the lever dislodged from the gunk that was blocking it and began to move. With one last effort, Frazz yanked it all the way down, and the ship's engines screamed to life.

"That's it!" barked Grunfloz. "I've got it! Now, let's take it down easy!"

"Arrrrrrgh!" Frazz slowly pushed the lever back up. Grunfloz gently lowered the garbage-gatherer to the ground near the big building and collapsed on the console to catch his breath. After several seconds he lifted an eyestalk toward Frazz.

"Thanks," he muttered.

Exhausted, Frazz surveyed the sizzling control panels and coughed, then tucked his eyeballs inside their lids and took a moment to collect his thoughts. Slowly he opened his eyestalks and took a deep breath.

"Grunfloz."

"What?"

"DON'T EVER TRY THAT AGAIN!"

Lunchbox slowly got his bearings inside of the garbage-gatherer. He looked through the front window of the machine and realized it was lying on its side. Seeing the open window directly above him, he launched himself from the steering column and up into the daylight. He stood triumphantly atop his vanquished prey and howled with joy. He recognized the location. The Scwozzworts had dropped him right next to the loading platform! Lunchbox trotted across the side of the vehicle and hopped onto the dock. Several bags of garbage had fallen there, ready to be dragged in for processing.

Ah, my beautiful garbage! Time to get back to work!

23

"I still can't believe you hijacked a garbage truck," said Nate. "I know you can't drive!" Nate was drenched in sweat. He had removed his shirt and tie, but his undershirt and shoes were stained with smelly garbage.

Lunchbox leaped from the loading dock onto the side of the garbage truck. They had succeeded in getting all of the stray bags that had fallen around the parking lot. They seemed to keep appearing from out of nowhere. He tugged on a lever at the truck's side. With a grinding whine, the compactor slid open.

"You mean there's still more?" cried Nate, seeing at least another ton of smashed bags.

Lunchbox barked impatiently.

"Okay, I'm coming! *Geez!*" Nate climbed wearily down into the rear of the garbage truck. The opening was narrow, barely big enough for him to squeeze through with a bag of garbage. The smell was horrendous, like a hundred restaurant Dumpsters full of carrion. His dress shoes slipped on the slimy walls of the container. He was sure his mom would kill him. Still, they needed to get the garbage processed as fast as possible. It would be only a few hours before Mr. Purvis showed up with his cleanup crew, maybe sooner.

Grabbing two of the nearest bags, Nate hurriedly climbed out to where the air was reasonably fresh. He took a moment to look at the wheeled metal basket from the pressure cooker. It sat on the loading dock with a fresh load of garbage bricks. Lunchbox snatched one of the bags from his hand and dragged it to the machine, leaving a wet oozy stripe across the concrete, like a giant slug trail. Nate took a deep breath and held it, then climbed back down into the stinking truck for more bags. He didn't see the basket of bricks disappear from the dock in a flash of light.

Frazz leaned back in his command couch, watching with satisfaction as Grunfloz retrieved another container from the capture bay and rolled it toward the corridor leading to the cargo hold. He was certain that a few of the *froonga* bricks would probably make a detour into Grunfloz's

124

quarters but knew that there was more where that came from. He smacked his lips and discovered a few crumbs he had missed, which he immediately licked off. He hefted another brick from the panel beside him and eyed it wonderingly.

"This is without question the finest *froonga* in the universe!"

"Thaf nefinidely thrue," said Grunfloz, chewing two bricks at once. He swallowed greedily. "The cargo bay's filling up pretty fast now."

"We'd probably better pack extra, at the rate you're eating it!" Frazz smiled and popped a brick into his mouth.

"Buhhhhhhhhp," belched Grunfloz. "All we have to do is keep scanning the area for garbage containers, then pick them up and drop them near the platform. That way the creatures can stay busy making *froonga* for us."

Frazz patted his belly below his lips. He was almost back up to his normal weight. He decided to worry about rationing once he'd regained the lost mass. They would be able to completely restock the hold in a few more days, provided the two little creatures down there kept working without distractions.

A squishing sound near the communications panel interrupted Frazz's reverie.

"Oh, yuck," said Frazz out loud. "You again!"

"*B-b-b-blorp*," said the oozy thing from Furporis

Twelve. Before Frazz could get up to shoo it away, it extended little strings of itself and gooshed up the side of the communications console, quickly forming little appendages to punch the buttons and switches on the panel, and then slid down and gooped across the deck, heading back to its nest.

Frazz punched the intercom. "Grunfloz, that thing did it again!"

Grunfloz came lumbering back to the control cabin and quickly checked the coordinates of the sent transmission. As before, they were aimed at a region of space just beyond the edge of the solar system . . . except this time the "message acknowledged" light was blinking.

Grunfloz studied the panel quietly for a few minutes. "It's nothing to worry about," he said finally. "Just space noise. Yes. Solar wind, that's all."

Frazz felt the undigested *froonga* gurgle in his belly. "Solar wind."

"Yes, solar wind."

"And nothing to worry about," repeated Frazz.

"Absolutely nothing to worry about," Grunfloz assured him.

Frazz folded his tentacles tightly. "Fine . . . I won't worry . . ." He smiled with clenched teeth. "I'm not worrying . . . I'm not worrying . . ."

24

"**L**unchbox, we've got to go," said Nate. "It's getting late." He stuffed his shirt and tie into his backpack. "Besides, we're bound to have company here any minute. Mr. Purvis is gonna *freak* when he finds the garbage truck. And we *especially* don't want him to see *you* here."

"Hrrrrrrooommmm," complained Lunchbox. Fresh bags of garbage, as well as a large fast-food Dumpster, had recently appeared on the dock. Lunchbox grabbed another bag and dragged it to the machine.

"I'm tired!" cried Nate. "I also don't want to get in more trouble! Let's *go*!"

Lunchbox growled his disapproval and continued

cramming garbage into the chute. Nate shouted over the noise of the machine.

"Look, just because you think you're Superdog doesn't mean you can't get hurt! We need to go home now!" He pointed to the floor by his side. "Lunchbox! *Heel!*"

Lunchbox looked at him with a you've-got-to-be-kidding expression.

Nate yanked at the dog angrily. "Let's go!"

Lunchbox snarled, raising the hair on his back. Startled, Nate let go of him and backed away. With tears in his eyes, he shouldered his backpack, tugging on the straps much harder than necessary.

"Fine with me! Stay here with your stupid garbage and take your chances! I'm going home!" He yanked the exit door open, and then turned and yelled, "You care more about your weirdo space friends anyway!" Eyes stinging with tears and sweat, Nate started down the concrete steps. He took off his glasses and tried to wipe his eyes with his arm, but his arm smelled awful and made his eyes sting even more. He headed toward the side of the building, then suddenly stopped and ducked around the corner.

A short man from Purvis Sanitation was opening the gate for Mr. Purvis, who drove through in a battered pickup truck.

Nate scrambled back up the steps and shut the side door behind him.

"Lunchbox!" he hissed. "We've got company!"

Lunchbox ignored him and continued dragging garbage to the machine. Nate quickly rolled the loading dock door shut. Lunchbox turned and growled.

"Lunchbox, *shut up!*" Nate ran to the machine and switched it off, then clamped his hand on Lunchbox's collar. "Listen!" He could hear the pickup doors slam and the crunch of gravel as the intruders grew near. Lunchbox's ears perked up. He growled again.

"Be quiet or you'll get us killed!" Nate tiptoed to the side door and peered through the gap, giving him a clear view of the disabled garbage truck and the mess on the dock. The two men stopped as they rounded the corner of the building.

"What the—" said Purvis. "It's my missing truck!"

"Somebody knocked it over!" said the other man. He swatted at the flies that seemed fascinated by his grungy coveralls. Purvis walked slowly around the truck, stopping to peer in through the cracked front windshield to make sure there were no bodies.

"Check in the back, Manny," Purvis ordered.

"Aw, c'mon, boss, it smells like somebody died!"

"Maybe somebody did! You're a garbageman. Get in there and look, will ya!"

"Okay, okay, I'm checkin'!" Manny took a deep breath and squeezed into the gap made by the retracted compactor. He scrambled out quickly, gagging and waving flies away from his face. "It's empty!"

"No garbage?"

"No nothin'. Just stink."

"This is weird. Hey, where'd that Dumpster come from?"

"What Dumpster?"

"On the dock! That ain't s'posed ta be there!" Purvis unhooked his cell phone from his belt while Manny wandered near the steps.

Nate held his breath and pulled Lunchbox close. "Easy, boy," he whispered as Lunchbox's muscles tightened under his fingers. Nate massaged him gently. "Easy." Manny had started to climb the steps to the door when a flash of blinding light on the dock startled him. His mouth flopped open, but no sound came out.

Purvis had his back to them as he talked on his cell phone. "That's what I said, *yer honor!* Somebody dumped my truck here an' wrecked it!"

Manny looked particularly pale as he gestured frantically to get his boss's attention. Oblivious, Purvis continued ranting into the phone.

"The guys told me that psycho dog attacked again. . . . Well, of course it sounds crazy! Dogs don't drive, an' I know garbage trucks don't fly. . . . No, I *don't* know how it got here!" Purvis rubbed the top of his shaved head with his free hand. "No, I ain't gonna be able to get nothin' done here tonight—I gotta get a tow truck—probably with a crane—it's gonna cost me big time!"

Manny finally found his voice, though it cracked slightly. "Leland . . ."

Purvis covered the phone with his hand. "Not now, poot head! I'm talkin' to the mayor!"

"BOSS!" Manny blurted out.

"What? Can't you see I'm bus—where'd it go?"

"I don't know! It—it was here a minute ago, now it's not!"

"Mr. Mayor, I'll call ya back." Purvis snapped the phone shut. He looked to see if the Dumpster had fallen on the other side of the dock. It wasn't there.

Nate tightened his grip. He could feel the dog's pulse racing and knew that any second now Lunchbox was going to break free and complicate things even more. "Don't do it, boy," he whispered. "Don't *do* it."

Lunchbox wriggled loose and butted the door open with his head. He made a beeline for the garbagemen.

"*Barrrooooo!*"

"Oh, *no*, not again!" shouted Purvis, immediately putting Manny between himself and the raging basset.

"What're you doing, Leland! Lemme go!" cried Manny. "That dog's got rabies!"

Lunchbox bared his fangs.

Purvis kept a firm grip on his employee's shoulders. "No sudden moves, Manny. . . . Now, we're gonna walk backwards, real slow, real quietlike." He took a careful step back, pulling his trembling helper along. "Stay calm . . ."

Lunchbox inched toward them as they slowly side-stepped around the corner of the building. Purvis stole a glance at his pickup thirty yards away. "Okay . . . on three . . . we're gonna run for it. . . . One . . . two . . ."

A large Dumpster suddenly fell from the sky and landed on the pickup, crushing it to the ground with a deafening bang. Glass and garbage sprayed all over the parking lot.

". . . thr—*what the*—"

"Leland, let's get outta here!"

"I'm with ya!" The men sprinted for the open gate as Lunchbox unleashed his victory howl.

25

Grunfloz chuckled as he leaned back from the viewer. "*That* was fun."

"I think you could have been a little more subtle." Frazz sniffed. "You're going to attract too much attention."

"Listen, no unauthorized creature is going to get near our *froonga* machine. I'll do whatever's necessary until the hold is fully loaded."

Nate slept late the next morning and awoke feeling like he'd been run over by a garbage truck. He had used up all of the hot water the night before trying to get rid of the smell; he'd gone through half a bottle of shampoo and an entire gooey sliver of deodorant soap, leaving a bathtub ring of monumental proportions. The shrill interrogation from his mother over why he chose to wear his best clothes to play in the landfill had taken a lot out of him.

Lying was getting old. Wallowing in garbage was *really* getting old. He had woken up several times during the night, dreaming he was covered with sour milk shakes and pickle juice, being eaten alive by flies and cockroaches. Sometimes he dreamed the aliens were dropping a Dumpster on him.

And all for nothing. Nate had concluded that Mr. Carson was just being polite. What did an eleven-year-old kid know about business anyway? Setting up a corporation and courting investors wasn't exactly like building a lemonade stand in the driveway.

No, it wasn't going to work. Mayor Thornhill would succeed in buying the cannery, the garbage processor would be trashed, and the aliens would be really upset. Nate thought again about the computer slide show Lunchbox had made. The picture of Earth broken in pieces. . . . This was serious business.

Maybe the aliens planned to enslave the whole planet and put the humans to work in garbage mines, after brainwashing their dogs. Maybe the world really *was* going to the dogs.

Nate slowly put his clothes on and trudged out to the kitchen.

"Well, nice to have you back among the living," said his mother, with false cheerfulness. "After breakfast you can help me with your dirty laundry."

Nate flopped down at the table and stared at his cereal bowl, resting his cheeks on his hands. "Did Lunchbox come home?" he asked glumly.

"No, he didn't. I'm afraid you're going to have to chain him up. Several people have called, saying he's running all over town and getting into their trash."

"I thought he had help," muttered Nate.

"What?"

"Um . . . I said I'll help . . . with the laundry." Nate felt like banging his head on the tabletop. Another lie. With each lie he felt smaller and more like a criminal. All of the stories were due to unravel sooner or later. But the truth was even more outrageous. Yeah, Dad, Lunchbox and I used your inventions to build a garbage-processing machine so that we could keep an alien civilization from destroying the world.

The front door opened suddenly. Mr. Parker trudged in, carrying a cardboard box. He looked pale. Silently he sat down in his recliner and stared at the wall. Nate noticed that the box was full of family photos and a few books.

"You're home awfully early," said Mrs. Parker. "Are you okay?"

"No, I'm not," he mumbled. "Durwood fired me."

"*Fired* you! What for?"

"Fraternizing with the enemy."

Mrs. Parker sat down across from him and leaned forward. "What?"

Nate stayed at the table but trained his ears on his parents' conversation, letting the cereal go soggy rather than drown them out with his chewing.

Mr. Parker removed his glasses and closed his eyes, rubbing the bridge of his nose between his thumb and forefinger. "Durwood," he began, pausing to try to piece the incident together, "saw an e-mail on my computer from Pete Carson, and printed it." He pulled a crumpled piece of paper from the box and handed it to his wife.

She read it out loud. "'Mr. Parker: Amazing results! Let's discuss an offer.'"

"I have no clue what this is about," said Mr. Parker.

Nate jumped up and tossed the rest of his cereal into the garbage disposal. "I've got to go," he said as he yanked open the front door and dashed out to his bike.

26

Lunchbox proudly surveyed his production from the previous night. Ten more baskets of *froonga* had been filled and transferred to the *Urplung Greebly*, all without the boy's help.

My boy is too fragile. He should eat some froonga, he thought.

He yawned slightly and then sat down to calculate how much more garbage was needed to finish restocking the ship's hold. This was one of the days when people didn't put their garbage out. He'd have to wait until the next day, so he decided to go home and see how his boy was doing.

He carefully secured the rolling door after leaping up and catching the rope in his teeth. He fished around in the leftover inorganic trash until he found a plastic gro-cery bag. He lovingly placed a few *froonga* bricks in the bag and grasped the loops in his teeth. He didn't want to leave without taking along a snack. Then he hopped down the steps and trotted toward home.

"Why's it leaving?" cried Frazz. "It's not done yet!"

"I don't know," said Grunfloz. "It shouldn't leave the machine unguarded like that. Especially not now."

"Maybe it's looking for more garbage. Surely we can scan this planet and find all the garbage it needs!"

"We could—except for *that*." Grunfloz adjusted the scan to highlight two large vehicles moving toward the *froonga* building.

"More intruders! We've got to do something!" Frazz twisted his head tendrils around his eyestalks.

"Well, we can't pick them up, that's for sure," said Grunfloz. "We may have to resort to more drastic mea-sures." He leaned back on his couch and fixed his eye-stalks on Frazz, not saying anything for several minutes.

"Grunfloz, why are you staring at me?" Frazz slowly backed away, waving his tentacles in front of himself as if trying to ward off a swarm of *droob* flies.

"*Drastic* measures," said Grunfloz with a grim smile.

Nate was nearing total panic as he pedaled toward the cannery. Mr. Carson was nowhere to be found. His secretary said he was out of the office for the rest of day and would be back after the holiday weekend.

Nate gnashed his teeth. Mayor Thornhill would own the cannery by then. Without Mr. Carson, all was lost.

Nate slowed as he turned onto Industrial Street. A wrecker pulled out of the cannery's front gate with the flattened remains of Mr. Purvis's pickup. Through the fence, Nate could see a much larger wrecker noisily winching the garbage truck up onto its wheels. Mr. Purvis and Manny stood in the parking lot. Purvis was waving his arms, apparently arguing about the price with one of the wrecker crewmen. Nate spun the bike around and raced for home.

"Me? Why *me*?" gasped Frazz in alarm. "Why not you?"

"Because you're the captain," said Grunfloz curtly.

"But that means I can order *you* to go down there."

"Someone has to stay aboard and monitor the systems, and you don't know how." Grunfloz finished assembling the mission harness and held it up in front of Frazz. "Now, this has your comlink, first-aid kit, emergency breather, and, most importantly, *this*." He carefully drew a crystal-tipped cylinder from its holster.

"A stun-zapper?" cried Frazz. "I've never *used* one of those things."

"Just be sure that if you do use it, *this* end is pointed at your target."

"I know *that*," said Frazz, rolling his eyestalks until they almost knotted around each other. "But do you really think I'll have to use it?"

"If you're careful and stay out of sight, you shouldn't have a problem. I'll be monitoring everything from up here and can alert you to any danger."

"But what am I supposed to *do* down there?"

"Guard the machine until the creature comes back. Deal with any intruders."

"*Intruders?* Forget it, no way! I'm not going down there. *You* do it!"

"Sorry, *sir.*" Grunfloz cinched the harness tightly around Frazz, then picked him up bodily and tossed him into the capture bay's air lock, slamming the door shut before he could turn around and run out.

Frazz pounded on the window, his shouting muffled by the thick material. Grunfloz switched on the intercom. Frazz's high voice crackled through the speaker.

"—that you get the *eebeedee* for mutiny! You'll never get away with—"

"Frazz! Listen! There's one more thing you need to know!" Grunfloz shouted.

"What, that you can't wait to shoot me out of the air lock and watch me explode?"

"*Sir!* If you can't protect the machine—"

Frazz stuck the tips of his tentacles into his auditory nubs and shouted. "*La la la la la la!* I'm not listening!"

"*Malfurbum gwealfee,*" muttered Grunfloz. He tapped the specimen stun-grid, which sent a mild jolt through the floor of the capture bay.

"Owww!" Frazz hopped involuntarily.

"Now, shut up and listen!" barked Grunfloz. "If you *can't* protect the machine, you will have to *destroy* it!"

"Destroy our *froonga* machine? Are you *furmnorkle*?"

"We can't risk a chain reaction if they damage the *plookie* regulator! Got that?"

"Yes! No! *Wait!*"

Grunfloz sighed in disgust and activated the force bubble. In an instant, the floor opened up, and the beam with Frazz encased in it shot to the planet below.

27

Immediately after Nate arrived home to find Lunchbox safe and sound, his parents led him into the den and sat him down on the small leather couch with his mother on one side and his father sitting in his computer chair, pulled up so close to the couch that their knees were almost touching. He decided there was nothing left to lose by telling the whole truth, no matter how weird it sounded.

After about an hour Mr. Parker was ripping his hair out in clumps.

"Nate, I've heard enough about space aliens and superintelligent dogs! Lunchbox is an ordinary basset hound! He doesn't know *anything* about physics, or engineering, or computers! He's a *dog*! He does *dog* things—chasing cars, digging in garbage—"

"So he can manufacture food for the aliens," insisted Nate. "And it's the best dog food in the world! Ask Mr. Carson!"

"It was your little venture with Mr. Carson that cost me my *job* today," snapped Mr. Parker. "And your dog's wild behavior sure didn't score any points!"

"Dad, I'm telling the truth! I was only trying to help!"

"Help who? Me? Some help!"

"Help you, help Lunchbox, and help the aliens!"

"Son, there are *no aliens*!" Mr. Parker rose from his chair and paced around the den, rubbing his neck again.

"How do you *know* there are no aliens?" asked Nate defiantly.

"Because I know! Why would beings from another planet come all the way to Earth just to focus all their attention on one stupid dog?"

"Lunchbox isn't stupid!"

The television suddenly began blasting at full volume in the living room, shaking the walls with snippets of two dozen channels in rapid succession. Mr. Parker yanked the door open and shouted, "Lunchbox! Turn that down, we're trying to talk in here!"

Lunchbox, sprawled in Mr. Parker's favorite recliner, clumsily pawed the remote control until the volume dropped to a whisper.

"That's better!" Nate's dad turned back toward his chair. "Now, where was—" He stopped in midstride, his mouth wide open.

"Um . . . Connie, what just happened?" he asked nervously. Mrs. Parker shook her head, speechless.

Nate smiled smugly. "Something wrong?"

"I can't believe he sent me down here in broad daylight," Frazz whimpered. He stood frozen to the spot, too terrified to move. Grunfloz had dropped him in the tall weeds near the fence that surrounded the big building. Strange smells assaulted him. He fumbled with his emergency breather, certain that the atmosphere was poisonous to Scwozzworts. Little winged things hopped out of the vegetation and rasped at him. The bright sunlight made him squint.

Grunfloz's voice crackled through the comlink. "Frazz, do you read me?"

"I'm here," whispered Frazz. "And it's hot! Get me out of here!"

"I can't do that. Stay in the weeds until the vehicles leave. Then get inside the building and guard the *froonga* machine!"

"How am I supposed to do that without being seen?" Frazz hunkered down in the weeds as the big vehicle roared through the gate, pulling the battered garbage-gatherer behind it. A cloud of black exhaust smoke surrounded him. He took a few frantic gasps from his emergency breather.

"Don't waste your air, *sir*," said Grunfloz. "The atmosphere is relatively safe."

"*Relatively*? What does that mean, that it's just going to kill me less quickly?" Frazz coughed and made little gagging sounds.

Grunfloz's voice took on a more sarcastic tone. "You know, it's *so* nice and quiet up here—I could *really* get used to this."

"Aaaarrrrrrggh! All right, all right, I'm moving!" Frazz poked his eyestalks up from the weeds and scanned the area. No other creatures were in sight, except for little crawly ones and flying things that hovered around him as if he were covered in garbage himself. Frazz swatted at them with his tentacles and then sprinted across the open area toward the side of the loading platform. The planet's gravity tugged at him. Although Grunfloz had told him that it was less than that of their home planet, fifteen years in artificial gravity had taken its toll. Frazz was hyperventilating by the time he reached the platform. He took another gulp from his emergency breather.

"They never prepared me for this in accounting school," he panted. The heat on that side of the building was nearly unbearable. He ducked down beside the platform, bobbed his eyestalks up, and peered carefully inside. In the darkness he could see the dim flashing lights of the

plookie regulator atop one of the strangest contraptions he'd ever seen.

Frazz's comlink beeped, followed by Grunfloz's voice.

"Hold your position, Frazz."

"Hold my position?" he hissed. "I'm roasting here!"

"Two bipeds are headed your way from point five-five-one."

"What does *that* mean?"

"They're coming from the other side of the platform! Didn't you ever learn directional grid terminology?"

Frazz curled up against the corner of the loading platform, trying to make himself as inconspicuous as possible—as if the creatures on this planet would call a quivering green and orange alien inconspicuous. He moved one eyestalk up carefully near the edge of the platform. The two bipeds came into view, a big heavy one and a smaller one. The big one was making a lot of noise, in a growly, rumbling voice. Grunfloz would like this one, thought Frazz. He squinted his eyelid to keep the dust out of it and watched through the slit as the two creatures climbed the steps on the other side.

"They're looking at the *froonga* machine," whispered Frazz into the comlink.

"Can you get in closer?" said Grunfloz.

"You mean, go *in* there?"

"Look, didn't I give you a stun-zapper?"

"You know," said Frazz with false cheerfulness, "once you get used to the heat down here, it's really not so bad—actually it's quite pleas—"

"Just get in there!"

Frazz groaned and switched off the comlink. He peered around the side of the entrance. The two creatures were facing the *froonga* machine—at least as far as Frazz could tell, they were facing it. For all he knew, they might have extra eyes in the back of their heads, like the Bleenobs on Gangus Five.

Trembling, he quietly pulled himself onto the platform, keeping his eyestalks pointed at the two creatures. He slowly reached for the stun-zapper and eased it from its holster. The smaller creature climbed onto the *froonga* machine while the larger one rummaged loudly through the garbage strewn about.

A row of long cylindrical containers sat a short distance from the entrance. The end of one was partially open. Frazz carefully calculated his sprint time, wrapping his tentacles tightly around the stun-zapper. *Three . . . two . . . one . . . now!*

With his hearts pounding, he dashed toward the cylinder and slipped inside. He moved his eyestalks around the hatch to see if the creatures had noticed. If they had, they didn't seem to care . . . or maybe they were waiting to trap him. All he knew was that he wished he were safely aboard the *Urplung Greebly*. I shouldn't be the one down here risking my life, he thought. It's not fair. I'm the captain, not Grun—

The smaller creature suddenly reached for the *plookie* regulator, apparently attracted by the flashing lights.

No . . . don't touch that, please. . . . Frazz carefully pointed the stun-zapper. Gritting his teeth, he pressed the Fire button. A brilliant flash of light and a sizzling jolt knocked him backward against the wall of the container. Just before passing out, he had a vague recollection of Grunfloz telling him which way he was supposed to point the weapon.

28

I don't understand this, Lunchbox thought. He sat glumly at the curb in the late morning sun. Where is all the garbage? I know my calculations are correct. He sniffed the air and strained his eyes to scan up and down the street. Don't these stupid people know it's garbage day?

Nate coasted his bicycle to the end of the driveway. "Lunchbox, it's the Fourth of July. There's no garbage pickup today. You'll have to wait until tomorrow." He beckoned the dog to follow him. "Come on! Mom and Dad said we could go watch the parade . . . as long as you behave yourself."

Lunchbox groaned and slowly plodded after him,

gradually picking up speed until he was trotting alongside the bike.

Nate felt happy for the first time in days. "You sure showed them last night! I wish I'd had a video camera to catch Dad's face when you did your slide show on the computer!" He weaved his bike back and forth playfully. "We've got time to go to the park before the parade starts. Come on, let's run!" Nate leaned over the handlebars and pedaled hard. Lunchbox matched his speed effortlessly.

I hope he's leading me to some more garbage, thought Lunchbox.

The park was decorated with flags and ribbons. Assorted booths offered smoked turkey legs, curly fries, hot dogs, and snow cones. The delicious smells made Nate wonder why any dog would prefer processed garbage bricks. He shrugged and pulled his Frisbee out. "Okay, Lunchbox, go long!" He gave the disk a hard fling. Lunchbox took off running, but ran past it toward the public trash can, which was already filling with picnic leftovers. He rose up on his hind legs and stuck his nose into the container, which was mounted in a metal frame-work attached to a short pole.

"No, Lunchbox! Today's a holiday! We're not work-ing!" Nate retrieved the Frisbee and threw it toward the dog. Lunchbox flopped down dejectedly as the disk passed over him. "Come on, it's not that hard," shouted Nate. "It's easier than catching garbage trucks!"

150

Lunchbox cocked his ears as a strange banging and crashing sound started in the distance and quickly grew louder.

"Lunchbox, come on, the parade is starting!" Nate followed the growing crowd to the curb. Lunchbox made his way through the mass of legs until he caught up with him.

A fire engine slowly came into view at the head of the parade, its siren piercing the air. Lunchbox howled in pain. Firemen in their blue uniforms tossed handfuls of candy into the crowd. Next came the discordant sounds of the Mill Ferron High School Marching Ferrets. The band wore its summer parade uniform, which consisted of pretty much anything that was red, white, and blue, and comfortable enough to wear on the hottest day of the year. The blasting brass and pounding drums drowned out Lunchbox's howling. He tried to leave, but Nate held his collar.

"Don't run off, boy. Stay."

What kind of torture is this? No garbage, and all of this noise! Arrooooooo!

Following the band came the Mill Ferron cheerleaders, six skinny girls waving pom-poms and chanting what was apparently the only cheer they knew: *"Mill Ferron!* (CLAP, CLAP) *Go Team!* (CLAP, CLAP) *Mill Ferron!* (CLAP, CLAP) *Go Team!"*

The Ferret faithful in the crowd picked up the cheer, even though football season was still two months away, and soon everyone was chanting and clapping as the grand marshal's float came into view. *"Mill Ferron!* (CLAP, CLAP) *Go Team!"*

Nate had to work hard not to laugh. A small tractor pulled a large flatbed trailer. The whole trailer was wrapped in chicken wire, with wads of patriotically colored tissue paper crammed into the holes. Amid a sea of posters that read RE-ELECT THORNHILL stood the mayor himself, wearing an outrageously shiny Uncle Sam costume with a Dracula–style collar and cape. He waved and strutted, repeating the chant from the crowd.

Lunchbox cocked his ears. What's that they're saying? Mull heron. . . . No, that's not it. . . . Mule sterile . . . no feet? He listened again for the rhythm of the chant, and then looked at the figure on the trailer. A Scwozzwortian culture reference from *The Encyclopedia of Everything Else* came to his mind. Suddenly the chant made sense. *Malfurbum—Gwealfee! Malfurbum—Gwealfee!* It's that stupid person who destroyed our wagon! He's being punished for his crimes! He's doing the dance of stupidity! This is an *eebeedee!*

Lunchbox barked in rhythm with the crowd, doing his best to approximate the chant. *"Malfurbum* (ARF, ARF) *Gwealfee!"*

The float stopped in the middle of the street. The mayor picked up a bullhorn.

"Mill Ferron! Go Team!" he shouted. The crowd

bumped around him, waving flags and chanting louder as the mayor worked them to a fever pitch. He bounced around on the trailer like a fat middle-aged rock star. Nate suddenly noticed that Lunchbox was gone. He looked behind him but was unable to see through the mass of legs and arms and bellies in his way.

The crowd parted abruptly as a small dark shape shoved its way through it about ten yards to Nate's right.

"Oh, no! Lunchbox! NO! NO!"

Dragging a pilfered bag of garbage, Lunchbox ran into the street, where he tore the bag open and began flinging and kicking its contents at the man on the trailer. Lettuce, barbecue sauce, turkey bones, and mayonnaise flew through the air, peppering the mayor's shiny costume with multicolored splat marks.

"What the—mmmph!" A rotting watermelon rind caught the mayor across his mouth. Before he could recover, Lunchbox leaped onto the trailer and grabbed the shiny cape in his teeth.

Time to remove the *yakayaka*!

Lunchbox tugged hard on the cape, causing the mayor to gag and fall over as the collar tightened around his neck. Women and children screamed, and people swarmed around the trailer or ran away in panic.

"Lunchbox! Stop!" Nate shouted, trying to fight his way through the crowd. Lunchbox continued tearing at the costume, exposing the mayor's underwear.

153

"Mad dog!" somebody shouted. "Mad dog!"

"Clear the way!" Three police officers and several firemen shoved their way through the crowd and leaped onto the float. One of the cops reached for his pistol; another waved him off. "Put that away, Bill! You might hit the mayor!" He grabbed his lapel microphone and shouted for Animal Control.

"Lunchbox!" Nate reached the edge of the trailer and tried to pull himself aboard, but one of the firemen grabbed him by the arm and spun him away.

"Stay out of the way, kid! That dog's nuts!"

"No he's not! He's mine!"

One of the firemen and a cop threw a heavy padded blanket over the dog and wrestled him away from the mayor. Lunchbox squirmed and snarled beneath the blanket.

"Give us a hand here, guys!" shouted the officer. "He's too strong!" Four men pulled the blanket tightly around Lunchbox while another tied ropes around the blanket. They set their bundle on the ground and held it firmly to keep Lunchbox from wriggling free.

The crowd parted again as the Animal Control truck, horn blaring and blue lights flashing, pulled alongside the mayor's float. The driver jumped out and shouted an order to the men holding Lunchbox. They lifted him quickly and shoved him into the open cage on the side.

The dog-catcher slammed the aluminum door shut while the crowd cheered.

Nate stood helplessly at the curb, tears streaming down his face, screaming at the men to let Lunchbox go. The fireman who had shoved him out of the way wiped the sweat from his brow and frowned at him.

"I'm sorry, kid! You shoulda kept him home!"

Nate set his jaw and glared at him.

The fireman spoke a little more softly. "Listen, they're gonna take him to the pound and check him for rabies."

"He's had his shots!" shouted Nate. "They can't throw him in the pound!"

"Oh yes they can, sonny! He just attacked somebody—the mayor, of all people. I hate to tell ya this, but he's as good as dead. I'm sorry." The fireman turned and moved to help the paramedics who were checking the mayor for injuries. Nate balled his fists and stared at them through his tear-fogged glasses, feeling every muscle in his body tighten. With rage and panic boiling over, he turned and shoved his way through the gawking audience, ran to his bicycle, and took off in pursuit of the truck.

Frazz had no idea what time it was; it was completely dark inside of the big metal cylinder. He didn't know how long he'd been knocked out.

He gingerly opened the hatch and poked an eyestalk

out of the side. No creatures were visible, but what he saw nearly made him faint. He fumbled for his comlink.

"Grunfloz, come in!"

"It's about time! Where have you been?"

"Grunfloz! The *plookie* regulator! It's gone!"

29

Nate tugged at the straps of his backpack as he climbed off his bike. The late afternoon sun streamed across the flat roof of the county animal shelter, nearly blinding him. Inside he could hear several dogs barking, though none of them sounded like Lunchbox. Despite the heat, his sweat was cold in his palms. Lunch-box could already be dead.

Nate swallowed back any more thoughts about it and focused on what he had come to do. Forgetting his fear and exhaustion, and knowing that the fate of the world might rest in his hands, he trudged up the walk, his feet feeling like lumps of lead, and grasped the steel door handle.

Locked! Nate surveyed the dusty parking lot. One patrol truck, one beat-up old sedan. Nate pounded hard on the door. The blinds covering its small window parted, showing an eyeball and some greasy hair through the slit.

"Sorry, kid, we're closed," came a muffled voice through the door.

"I want to see my dog!" shouted Nate. No response. Nate kicked the door several times. This time the knob turned, and the door opened a crack, just wide enough for the tall, skinny young man inside to stick his head out.

"I said we're closed!" He wore an exaggerated Elvis–style haircut and a ring through his eyebrow. A half-burned cigarette dangled from his lower lip. Nate didn't budge. The man stuck a wiry, tattooed arm through the door and poked his tobacco-scented finger an inch away from Nate's nose. "Go home, punk."

"Not until you let me see my dog."

The man sighed. "Which one?"

"The basset hound."

"*That* one. Tough luck, kid. The vet's gonna put him to sleep tomorrow."

"You can't do that!" cried Nate. "He doesn't have rabies!"

"He doesn't have to. Vicious dogs are destroyed. It's the law."

"He's not vicious," insisted Nate. "*Stupid*, maybe, but not vicious. Let me see him." Nate stepped inside, wrinkling his nose at the combination of disinfectant and dog smells.

"Fine, but no long good-byes, okay? I got a lotta work to do."

Nate headed for the doors to the kennel, big, wooden, swinging double doors with windows in them.

"Hold it there, kid."

"What?"

The keeper held his hand out. "Your backpack. I don't think I can trust you."

Nate sighed and handed him the backpack. The young man unzipped it and began to rummage through it. "Phew! When was the last time you washed this—hey, waaaaitaminute. What's this?" He pulled a wooden-handled object from the pack. "A hacksaw!" He smirked at Nate and shook his head.

Nate rolled his eyes. "You really think I'm that stupid? It's for a Scout project."

"Sure. Nice try, kid. Betcha got some bolt cutters in here, too."

"Yeah, *right*. Can I just go see my dog already?"

"Two minutes. And I'll be watchin' you." The keeper pushed the door open and let Nate through. It really stunk in the kennel. Nate passed by the rows of steel cages. Little dogs yapped and shrieked; big dogs woofed and snarled; puppies looked at him with wet brown eyes and begged for attention. At the far end, across from a cage that held an enormous, slobbering boxer-mastiff mix, sat Lunchbox, moping and looking unusually droopy, even for a basset.

At the sight of Nate he thumped his tail slightly, but he still looked sad and confused.

"I hope you're proud of yourself," said Nate loudly. He glanced behind him. Through the smudged windows the keeper stared suspiciously. Nate gave him a "what?" shrug and showed his open palms. He turned to Lunchbox and knelt down by the cage.

"Listen to me, bonehead. You've really done it this time. You may be the smartest dog on the planet, but that was really *dumb*. Dumb dog!"

Lunchbox whined, not really understanding the words but recognizing the tone of voice. He looked behind him where he had soiled the concrete floor.

"Not that, stupid!" said Nate. "You don't know how much trouble you've gotten us into—Dad lost his job, the mayor's probably gonna sue us, and tomorrow you're getting the needle."

The phone in the outer office rang. The keeper hesitated, then moved to answer it.

Quickly Nate's voice dropped to a whisper. "I brought you something. Here." He pulled a large file from under his shirt and slid it between the steel bars. "Shhh! He's coming back!"

Lunchbox flopped down on top of the file and thumped his tail knowingly.

The keeper pushed the door open. "Sorry, kid, time's up. Maybe you'd like to adopt a new puppy?"

Nate frowned at the sorry collection of mutts and shook his head.

"No. I'd rather have a hamster." He pushed past the young man, retrieved his backpack from the desk, and slammed the front door behind him. Once in the parking lot, he jumped on his bike and willed his aching legs to pedal him back up the road into town. "This better work," he said under his breath.

Lunchbox cocked his ears, filtering out the noise from the other dogs, waiting until he heard the man flop into his seat in the office. These fools aren't loud enough. He looked over at the big ugly dog across the aisle. "Hey! Hey, you! Hey! Hey! Hey!" Lunchbox barked. Not to be outdone, the big dog responded.

"Hey! Hey! Hey! Hey!"

Lunchbox picked up a mouthful of stale kibble and spat it through the bars at the sleeping dog next to him, hitting it squarely between the eyes. Startled, it jumped up on its long spindly legs and joined the conversation.

"Hey! Hey! Hey! Hey!"

Soon all of the dogs picked up the chant until the noise was deafening. The keeper stuck his head through the door and yelled something Lunchbox recognized: *"Shut up!"* Seeing that it had no effect, the man shook his head and closed the door.

"Everybody! Hey! Hey! Hey!" Lunchbox continued to stir up the other dogs. "Barrrooooo! Barrrooooo! Louder, you morons! That's it!"

Carefully, he picked up the file in his teeth and began sawing.

30

"**H**ow could you *lose* the *plookie* regulator?" Grunfloz shouted so loudly that the comlink vibrated in Frazz's tentacle. "You were supposed to guard the machine, *sir!*"

Frazz heard the sound of alien babbling outside. "Grunfloz! Something's coming!"

"Looks like those same two coming your way!" barked Grunfloz.

"Can't you just bring me up?" cried Frazz.

"No! You've got to find the *plookie* regulator!"

"Can't you just scan for it?"

"I already tried! Better charge up your stun-zapper— *carefully!*"

The stun-zapper! Oh, no! Where did I leave it? Frazz worried.

Frantically, Frazz brushed his tentacles around the area, trying to see if it had fallen from its holster. He stretched his eyestalks down to look under the machinery, but all he got were eyeballs full of dust and sticky strands of something really scary. He scrubbed the goo out of them, slapping at the little eight-legged thing that came with it.

The two creatures entered the building cautiously. The bigger one growled a lot, checking the power connections carefully and gesturing for the smaller one to pick up the garbage surrounding the *froonga* machine. Frazz held his breath. Please, oh, please, don't turn it on! he silently pleaded.

The big one walked around the machine, inspecting its construction, then pulled what was apparently a communication device from its belt. It walked outside to the platform. The smaller one looked around nervously and began stuffing garbage into the intake chute of the *froonga* machine. Frazz groaned. He knew what he had to do next.

As the creature reached for the power switch, Frazz swallowed hard, turned bright orange, and dashed toward it, waving his tentacles as he ran.

"EEEEEEEEEEEYYYYYAAAAAAAAAAAAAAGH!" he shrieked.

The creature dropped the garbage and ran screaming

toward the exit. Frazz pursued it through the door, leaping down the metal steps after it.

I must be insane, Frazz thought, and stopped near the fence, ducking back into the weeds where he'd started out. The smaller creature raced down the street. The larger one came around the side of the building to see what all the racket was about, still talking into its communicator thing. Frazz knew he needed to keep it from the *froonga* machine but wasn't sure how. Despite Grunfloz's efforts to scare it off, it was back. Without a stun-zapper, another frontal attack wouldn't be wise. The creature was nearly as big as Grunfloz.

As he cowered in the weeds contemplating his next move, a large black vehicle rolled down the street and through the gate. It stopped by the building, and an even taller biped climbed out and went inside.

"Grunfloz!" Frazz whispered into his comlink. "Grunfloz, come in! Grunfloz, where are you?"

Lunchbox ignored the taste of metal filings in his mouth as he sawed through the last bar. The dogs that had already been freed continued their mindless barking, romping about and scuffling with one another. The big ugly dog woofed deeply to encourage him. The file clanged to the floor, and the huge animal butted the cage open, drooling all over him to show its gratitude.

Lunchbox eyed the big swinging doors. None of the

frolicking dogs had thought to push them open. With a mighty howl, he led the charge through the doors and into the room where the skinny man reclined with his feet on the desk. The man shouted and fell backward to the floor, then scrambled for the front door. Lunchbox gave chase, followed by the rest of the pack. The man ran to his vehicle, which was quickly surrounded by dogs. Lunchbox sounded his victory howl and sprinted up the road toward town.

As the sun slipped behind the trees, Nate pedaled into the center of town, exhausted. A crowd had begun to gather for the fireworks display. He turned his bike into the park, riding through the mass of people and picnic blankets. He scanned the faces desperately—everyone in town should be here. Where was Mr. Carson? Surely the politicians wouldn't miss this event.

Nate rode on, making several laps around the park. No sign of any of them. At the far edge of the park, he could see a group of boys throwing a glow-in-the-dark Frisbee. There were five of them. As he got closer, his heart nearly stopped. The disk didn't just glow, it pulsated. That was no Frisbee!

Nate slipped behind a hedgerow and watched. He recognized one of them as Warren Purvis, the most obnoxious kid in town, son of the garbage boss.

"Man, this is the coolest birthday present ever!" shouted Warren.

Nate shuddered, remembering Lunchbox's last slide show. These guys had no idea what kind of danger they were putting the world in! He pedaled at full speed toward them. It was dark enough now that they wouldn't see him right away.

Warren aimed a high pass toward one of his friends. Just as the boy turned to run and chase it, Nate maneuvered his bike under the disk and leaped from the crossbar.

"Hey! Stop that kid!" yelled Warren.

Nate tucked the disk into his arms, feeling its cold smoothness. It was thicker than a Frisbee, but very lightweight.

He picked his bike up and took off, leaving the crowd of shouting boys in his wake.

Lunchbox kept to the back streets, away from the park, and with his *froonga*-enhanced speed and knowledge of shortcuts, soon arrived near the big building. He sniffed the air, then put his nose to the ground by the entrance. He could smell intruders. Another smell reached his nostrils from the weeds by the fence. It was a very familiar smell, one that he could not easily forget. He ran across the moonlit parking lot, following the scent as it grew stronger.

The little whiny animal! He charged into the tall grass, startling it with his cold nose.

"*EEEEEEEEEEE!*" Frazz popped up from the weeds, waving his tentacles. "Don't *do* that! Listen!" Frazz was nearly glowing orange. "We've lost the *plookie* regulator. I chased one creature away, but now there are two creatures in there trying to start the *froonga* machine!"

Lunchbox growled and ran toward the building. Frazz ran after him, his thick round feet thumping the ground with each step. "We've got to stop them!" he shouted. "Hurry!"

Before Frazz could make it to the building, a circle of bright light surrounded him. He felt his body go rigid; his stomach seemed to drop to his feet as he was instantly yanked from the planet's surface.

The light quickly faded to reveal the *Urplung Greebly's* capture bay. Frazz shook his tentacles as he came out of the air lock. "Why did you have to bring me back *now*? I was just getting it under control!"

Grunfloz didn't turn around but bobbed an eyestalk back to look at Frazz. "We're under attack!"

"So? We've got a full-scale emergency down there, and the creature needs my help!"

"We've got a full-scale emergency here!" said Grunfloz breathlessly. "Uh-oh! *Incoming!*" Before Frazz could brace himself, the ship shuddered. Sparks and smoke flew from various conduits around the control center. The deck bucked for a moment, knocking Frazz off balance.

"Space noise! Solar wind!" he shouted as he scrambled to his feet. *"Absolutely nothing to worry about!"*

Grunfloz shoved Frazz out of the way as he ran across the deck to fumble with the attitude controls. "Why didn't you destroy the *froonga* machine?" He leaped out of the way of a sparking conduit. "The stun-zapper has a full blast setting!" He leaped over a fallen support beam and hurried to stabilize the engines.

The power grid suddenly exploded, hurling Grunfloz across the cabin into the far wall; the *Urplung Greebly* tumbled end over end, bouncing both Scwozzworts around in a cloud of flying debris as the gravity generator failed.

Lunchbox cornered the fat, stupid garbageman, snarling viciously. The other man, the *malfurbum gwealfee* he had attacked earlier that day, shouted at the fat man and climbed on top of the *froonga* machine. He yanked a metal support rod from the machine and tossed it to the fat man, shouting something that sounded like *hitem*, or *gitem*.

Lunchbox dodged as the fat man swung the rod; it whooshed past his ears. He started to leap at him, but the man swung again, stinging him in the ribs. He howled in pain, but landed on his feet and turned to attack again.

The man ran close to the open hatch of one of the long metal cylinders.

"Come on!" he shouted. Lunchbox dashed toward the man, who suddenly pulled the hatch open wider and swung the rod again. Lunchbox leaped out of the way and landed inside of the cylinder, sliding on the greasy bottom. Quickly the man slammed it shut, leaving the dog in total darkness. Lunchbox ran toward the noise and slammed his head against the door. It made bright lights pop in his head, but he continued pushing and clawing, snarling and howling at the top of his lungs.

He suddenly stopped barking as a rumbling noise from outside sent a chill through his body. . . .

Someone was starting up the *froonga* machine!

Frazz painfully looped a tentacle around the damaged control console and pulled the unconscious Grunfloz down with the other. He felt like he was going to *rurfroo* as the *Urplung Greebly* continued to tumble.

"Grunfloz! Wake up! Stay with me!"

Frazz pulled him tighter to keep him from floating away. He glanced through the view screen at the changing scenery. The *Urplung Greebly* was apparently rotating laterally as well as end over end. It was a dizzying sight, seeing first the stars, then the blue, brown, and white planet below, then the planet's moon in the distance, then the stars again, then a large black shadow . . .

170

The ship suddenly stopped turning as the black shadow came into view; Frazz held on tightly to Grunfloz and the control panel to keep from floating. As the dark ship approached, an array of flashing lights appeared around its perimeter. A long black tube slowly extended toward the *Urplung Greebly*'s main air lock.

The little oozy thing from Furporis Twelve propelled itself through the smoke and trash in the cabin and splattered against the view screen, obstructing Frazz's sight of the black ship. It glorped and burbled excitedly.

"Well, at least *one* of us is happy," said Frazz wearily. "It can't get any worse."

An emergency honker blared above the main scanner screen, one of the few things that still appeared to be working. Above a pulsating graphic that showed its location and projected time remaining, bright purple letters blazed the words "DANGER! PLOOKIE WAVE DETECTED!"

Lunchbox shook his head, trying to make the little lights go away. He closed his eyes until they disappeared, hearing the whine of the *froonga* machine as it processed fresh garbage. He could hear the two men laughing and shouting.

Disoriented, Lunchbox could still see one very small pinpoint of light. He closed his eyes; it disappeared. He opened them again, and it was back. Something was flashing at the far end of the tube! He scrambled toward it. Skidding to a halt in front of it, he recognized the

Scwozzwortian symbols for up and down; the light was at the down position. Another reference from *The Encyclopedia of Everything Else* came to him. A stun-zapper! Lunchbox quickly seized the long weapon in his teeth and ran to the front of the tube with it. Wedging it with the crystal end against the latch mechanism, he pawed at the control button, holding it down until the light glowed brightly at the "full blast" position. He dashed to the rear of the chamber and curled up tightly, tucked his long ears under his paws, and closed his eyes.

Grunfloz slowly opened his eyestalks. It took some effort to keep them from bobbing around in the weightless environment. "What happened?" he asked weakly.

"Oh, nothing much," said Frazz flatly. "Some mysterious black ship blew out the capture beam and most of the ship's critical systems, a hostile alien boarding party is on its way, and there's a *plookie* wave building up on the planet below. Other than that, it's been pretty dull around here."

Grunfloz snapped awake, his eyestalks flying around his head in circles as they took in the damage and the flashing scanner. "We've got to get out of here!" he gasped.

"Too late," said Frazz. "The *Urplung Greebly* is dead in space. The boarding party is in for a big surprise—but they won't live long enough to notice it."

"So this is it, huh?" Grunfloz noticed that Frazz's head tendrils were a relaxed green color, waving gently.

"I'm afraid so, Grunfloz. I'm sorry. I was really hoping I wouldn't have to go out as a—a—"

"A *malfurbum gwealfee?*" said Grunfloz, wincing as he massaged a bruise on the side of his head. "I don't think so."

"Thanks, but I don't believe you. That's your favorite insult."

"It's only an insult because you believe it."

"It's true," sighed Frazz. "I can't do anything right."

The *plookie* warning increased its intensity. Grunfloz wrapped a bruised tentacle gently around Frazz's.

"You gave it your best. You tried really hard to be a good captain."

"So you think I'm a good captain after all?"

"No, you really stink at it." Grunfloz smiled sadly. "But you never quit trying."

Frazz returned the squeeze and the bittersweet smile. "Not much time left, old friend." The *plookie* warning doubled its frequency, its flashing light creating a strobe effect on the Scwozzworts' waving head tendrils.

"It was fun traveling with you, sir."

They closed their eyes tightly and wrapped their tentacles around each other, waiting for the end of everything.

31

Nate pedaled through the pain in his muscles, riding now for the whole world. As he turned onto Industrial Street, he could see lights glowing from the windows of the cannery. He skidded his bike through the open gate and made his way toward the loading dock at the side of the building. As he stumbled up the steps, he heard a familiar rumbling sound. The garbage machine! A strange red light began to radiate from the center of the machine; the arcing ring of current changed its color to match. The machine started to shake from its moorings; a bolt in the floor popped, sending little chunks of concrete through the air.

Leland Purvis and Durwood Thornhill stood at opposite ends of the machine, Purvis feeding garbage from a bag into the chute at one end, Thornhill watching in fascination as the bricks came out of the other end.

"It's recycling, yer honor! We can turn all this garbage into fertilizer and make a bundle!" shouted Purvis above the din. Nate ran toward them, shrieking.

"Turn it off! It's gonna blow the whole world up!"

Purvis snarled; Thornhill looked at Nate with disgust. "Buzz off, Nat!"

Nate started to run toward the machine, feeling for the holes in the bottom of the disk. He glanced up at the four conduits poking up from the center of the machine where the device should have been docked.

A sudden orange flash erupted at the end of the pressure cooker that stood just behind the garbage chute; the door swung open, knocking Purvis to the ground. A black, brown, and white missile shot from the inside. It sprang off his back and into the air as he tried to get up. Purvis hit the concrete face-first.

At the same moment, Nate felt someone grab his ankle and yank his leg straight behind him.

"Gotcha!" snarled Warren.

"Lunchbox!" Nate yelled at the airborne dog, flinging the disk as hard as he could before tumbling painfully onto his knees and elbows.

With his ears flying behind him, Lunchbox leaped for the glowing device as gracefully as any Jack Russell terrier.

He snatched it in his teeth, did a twisting front flip, landed on the scaffolding, and slammed the disk into its place. The red glow instantly subsided, and the arcing current around the machine returned to its whitish green color.

Lunchbox leaped from the scaffolding, knocking the mayor down, and ran, snarling, to place himself between Nate and Warren. Warren obligingly backed up. Nate got up and staggered to push the Stop button with his thumb and held it for a couple of seconds. The garbage machine groaned to a halt. A faint haze and smell of burned metal drifted through the air, dimly illuminated by the overhead lights.

Flashing strobe lights appeared outside; Nate heard the crunch and pop of tires sliding on gravel. Three police officers charged in from the loading dock with their guns drawn.

"We got a report of some illegal fireworks here," said the lead officer. Two of the cops trained their guns on Lunchbox. Nate ran and put his arms around the dog, glaring at them. Mayor Thornhill climbed to his feet and slowly walked toward the officer, his hands extended in greeting.

"Howard! Am I ever glad to see you!"

"Sir, what's going on?" The officer wrinkled his nose at the burned garbage smell.

"We've got trespassers and vandals here in my building," said Thornhill.

A loud and certain voice broke the air. "That's not quite true, Durwood."

Mr. Carson entered from the steps by the loading dock, followed by Nate's parents. A man in a very expensive suit brought up the rear.

"Pete! What on Earth are you doing here?" Thornhill blurted out.

"Well, Mr. Mayor, I'm taking possession of *my* building."

The mayor laughed. "I don't think so." He gestured to the man in the nice suit. "We've already worked out a deal for this property. Right, Dave?"

The lawyer shook his head. "I'm sorry, Mr. Thornhill, but I've been retained to act in the best interests of the seller, and, well, quite frankly, Mr. Carson's offer just blew yours out of the water."

Thornhill's face turned bright red; the veins on his forehead were visible. "You can't do that! We had a deal!"

"We had . . . a *verbal* agreement, nothing more. Mr. Carson has already signed the contract and secured the proper financing."

Mr. Carson smiled smugly. "That makes you a trespasser on *my* property, your honor." He turned to the policeman in charge. "Howard?"

Thornhill looked like his head would explode. "You can't do this! I'm the mayor of this town, not a common criminal!"

Nate could no longer contain himself. "He *is* a crook!"

"Nate," said his father. Mr. and Mrs. Parker each put a hand on his shoulders. "Calm down."

"It's true! I overheard him and Mr. Purvis! He's taking bribes!"

Thornhill sputtered angrily. "Boy, you don't have a clue what you're talking about!"

"It's true!" shrieked Nate. "You promised to renew Mr. Purvis's contract if he'd pay you 10 percent!"

Thornhill looked at the mess in the building and sneered at Purvis, who was massaging his bloody nose. "Why would I take bribes from this idiot? He can't even keep track of his garbage trucks! I've got a great bid from another company just waiting to go to the city council for approval! Ten percent. Ha!"

"It was twelve-and-a-half," snapped Purvis. "And I ain't no idiot. . . . *Oops.*"

Mr. Carson looked at the officer and cocked his head toward the mayor and the garbageman. "Well?"

Howard bit his lip and reached for his handcuffs.

"You're kidding, right?" said Thornhill, panic rising in his voice. "This is all your fault, Gerald! You set me up! You and your kid and that killer dog!"

Mr. Carson glared at the officers, who still had their guns trained on Lunchbox. "Gentlemen, I hope you're not planning to shoot our honorary vice president of research and development."

Howard waved his men forward, toward Thornhill and Purvis. "Mr. Mayor, Leland, I'm afraid you're going to have to come with us."

"You can't do that! You don't have any evidence except for old big mouth here!"

"Believe me," said Mr. Carson. "The city council will look into this matter very thoroughly."

The lawyer smiled and followed the officers as they led the alleged conspirators out. "I don't want to miss the fireworks," he said.

A skyrocket boomed over the park, shaking the building's metal roof.

179

"Well, Gerald," said Mr. Carson. "Your stock certificates will be ready Tuesday. The board of directors can't wait to get the first batch for their own dogs." He slowly waded through the mess and admired the machine. "An amazing contraption. We'll give you all the support you need to build more."

Mr. Parker swallowed and nodded, recognizing remnants of his inventions. "Yes, thank you. I think."

"Lunchbox will help you, Dad," said Nate confidently.

Mr. Carson extended his hand. "This is really going to be fun . . . *partner!*"

Mr. Parker shook his hand, hesitantly at first, but then more firmly. He broke into a wide grin, the first really happy smile Nate had seen in weeks. "Yes . . . yes, Pete, it's going to be *fun!*"

Nate and his family stepped out onto the dock as the fireworks finale lit the sky.

Frazz shook with a mixture of relief and fear. Grunfloz had managed to restore power to the gravity generator, but the capture beam unit was permanently destroyed.

The *Urplung Greebly* shuddered again as the black ship finished its docking maneuver. Frazz stood in front of the air lock, resigned to face whatever came through.

The oozy thing from Furporis Twelve skittered excitedly at his feet, leaving a slime trail over his bruised and battered skin. Frazz ignored it, choking down the urge to *rurfroo*.

Something slapped repeatedly against the hatch. Frazz slid it open with a steamy hiss.

A huge black blob filled the hatchway. It bubbled and pulsated, forming elongated tentaclelike appendages to probe its way into the ship.

"B-b-b-b-b-b-b-b-b-braaaaaaauuuuuuggggghhhh," it boomed.

Frazz stepped back. Grunfloz limped to his side and stared.

The little oozy thing from Furporis Twelve let out a burbling squeal: *"Ma-ma!"*

The Scwozzworts gaped in awe as the little creature slid into the larger one and was engulfed by its formless mass.

The huge oozy thing from Furporis Twelve formed a long tentacle and shot it into the cabin, past the Scwozzworts, and down the corridor to the specimen bay, probing its way through cubicle after cubicle of strange life-forms.

"No, not my specimens!" protested Grunfloz.

"B-b-b-b-b-b-RRRRRRRRRAAAAAAAAAAA-UUUUGGGHH!" insisted the creature.

"Oh . . . well, never mind." Grunfloz smiled timidly.

As the creature withdrew its gooey tentacle into itself, a parade of life-forms followed it—walking carnivorous plants from the Woofoo sector, thousands of fat yellow Orknalian spit-bugs, flying things, crawling things; all of them streaming toward the hatch. The big blob moved part of itself out of the way as the liberated specimens entered the long black tube.

As the last tiny *droob* fly fluttered through the opening, the little oozy thing emerged from inside the big one. It zipped over to the Scwozzworts and positioned itself between them, chattering affectionately. Grunfloz reached down and patted what he presumed was its head. The creature burbled happily, then stretched itself over Frazz, wrapping him in a gooey hug.

"Ewww! Just kill me now," muttered Frazz. The little blob once again merged with the big blob, and they slowly slid out of the hatch, closing it snugly behind them.

"See, I *knew* it liked you," snickered Grunfloz.

"Well, now what?"

"You're the captain," said Grunfloz. "What's the word?"

Frazz took a deep breath. "Let's go home. We have enough *froonga* for a straight return trip. I'm willing to risk the *eebeedee* rather than wait around for those creatures to blow the planet up."

"Good idea," said Grunfloz, stealing one last look at the planet.

"Best speed, Lowly Enlisted Scwozzwort *First* Class Grunfloz." Frazz leaned back on his tattered command couch and closed his eyes, thinking of the creatures that had risked their lives for *froonga*.

"I'm going to miss them," said Grunfloz.

"Me, too," sighed Frazz.

The *Urplung Greebly* slowly turned itself away from the planet and moved out into the dark uncertainty of space.

Acknowledgments

Thanks:

To the Lone Star Nightwriters: Dan Case, Gretchen Craig, Julie Williams, Debbie Haskins, Michael and Susan Denney, Cate Murray, and, again, Berniece Rabe.

To my editor, Reka Simonsen, and my agent, Ethan Ellenberg, for liking weird stuff.

To Mom, for PBJs, clean underwear, Band-Aids, and forgetting about the time I—wait, never mind, you didn't know about that.

To Dad, for instilling the ambition. I know you can read this from up there.

To my loving, beautiful, and brilliantly talented wife, Lesli, who is looking over my shoulder at the moment.

To my children, Nathaniel, Jarrod, Alyssa, Jacob, and Margo—KNOCK IT OFF, I'm trying to work here!